LEGACIES

Following in the footsteps of Sherlock Holmes and Doctor John Watson come their twenty-first-century descendants, Sergeant Samuel Holmes and Doctor Jamesina Watson, great-grandchildren of their famous forebears, working for the London, California police force. In their first case together, the pair must investigate a series of mysterious murders where the bodies of the victims are apparently unmarked. In doing so, they uncover a sinister conspiracy from a very old enemy that threatens not only their own lives, but those of their families . . .

D1634569

STEVEN FOX

LEGACIES

Complete and Unabridged

LINFORD
Leicester

First published in Great Britain

First Linford Edition
published 2017

Copyright © 2016 by Steven E. Fox
All rights reserved

*A catalogue record for this book is available
from the British Library.*

ISBN 978–1–4448–3130–6

1897959 21

Published by
F. A. Thorpe (Publishing)
Anstey, Leicestershire

Set by Words & Graphics Ltd.
Anstey, Leicestershire
Printed and bound in Great Britain by
T. J. International Ltd., Padstow, Cornwall

This book is printed on acid-free paper

RENFREW DISTRICT ARTS AND LIBRARIES COUNCIL

1

The detective sergeant walked into the division's break room about fifteen minutes early for his shift. Normally the room was empty just before the beginning of the third shift. Tonight he saw the newest member of the Forensic Medical Examiners team sitting alone at a table, her eyes closed with half a cup of cooling coffee placed before her.

'Rough night?' He poured a cup of coffee for himself and sat down. 'Care for some company?'

'Not just rough,' she said, 'but long. This is the second case in less than ten days where the deceased showed no signs of violence, but the cause of death could not be natural.'

'That seems too strange to be called a coincidence.' He took a deep sip from his coffee cup. 'How do you know the deaths weren't natural?'

'Two young, apparently healthy, males

don't just drop dead in alleys not five blocks from each other. Both men were nicely dressed. There were no signs of physical trauma and nothing appeared to be missing from their pockets. Toxicology couldn't find anything in the fluid or tissue samples.' The young FME yawned, stood up and stretched. Sitting back down, she continued:

'There were no marks on either of the bodies. In fact the only thing they had in common, other than being dead under mysterious circumstances, was the broken blood vessels in their eyeballs.'

'That sounds like something that will be on the bulletin board in the detective room by the time I get there. By the way, I'm Detective Sergeant Samuel Holmes.' He held out his hand.

'My name is Jamesina Watson.' She took his hand in a strong clasp. 'Call me Jamie.'

'And I'm Sam.'

Samuel finished his coffee, got up and headed toward the detective room. There was a note on his computer to see the lieutenant.

He went to the lieutenant's office, knocked twice on the open door's frame. 'You wanted to see me?'

'Come in and sit down, Sam. I've got two unusual cases, and the captain thought that since we have our own Holmes and Watson, he should team you two up to solve them.'

The lieutenant gave Sam a look that said there was no getting out of the assignment.

'You and Doctor Watson will report to the small conference room at 0900 the day after tomorrow to be fully briefed and to get your schedules in sync. Meanwhile, study the files on these just-identified John Does.'

Sam had endured a lot of hazing during his early days at the academy. After his first fitness review, the hazing had begun to become remarks of grudging respect from both his instructors and his peers. After graduation, he had applied for a position on the London, California police force.

He felt that, in a city founded by British immigrants at the end of the nineteenth century, his name wouldn't stand out as it had in greater Los Angeles.

His academy record and level of competence as a rookie street cop had put him on the fast track for promotion. His scores for both the corporal's and the sergeant's exams had placed him at the top of the promotions lists. He was now the youngest sergeant of detectives on the force.

★ ★ ★

Jamesina Watson's supervisor walked over to her desk the next day and sat down.

'The deaths of those two young men are still bothering you, eh, Jamie?' he asked.

'I just can't help but feel that I'm missing something in the autopsy,' she replied. 'Medical school made it all seem so cut and dried. No more unknown causes of death.'

'We have come a long way since our great-grandparents' day.' The supervisor gave Jamie a cautious look. 'But there's still a lot about medicine that can surprise us. Well, it does me, at least.'

Jamie had graduated at the top of her class and had excelled during her residency. She had chosen to work for a small city police M.E. team, rather than for a well-established hospital like Cedars Sinai or Johns Hopkins. The supervisor had often wondered why, but gratefully accepted the gift of a brilliant young protégé.

The supervisor let out a sigh, then: 'Would you like the opportunity to study these cases full-time? Partnered with an up-and-coming young detective?'

'You mean, like *The X-Files*? I'm to be Dana Scully to his Fox Mulder?' Jamie laughed.

'No,' the supervisor responded. 'According to the captain, more like you're Doctor Watson to his Sherlock Holmes. He wants Sergeant Holmes to work with you on these deaths. Since they are so mysterious, the captain wants them treated as homicides for the time being. You and the sergeant have a meeting at nine a.m. tomorrow. Bring all of your notes. Be prepared for some in-depth questions. Holmes is supposed to be the boy wonder of the detectives. He's the youngest sergeant on the force.'

The next morning, Jamie took her file case into the designated conference room and sat down. Moments later, the captain and the lieutenant of detectives walked in, just ahead of the young sergeant she had met two nights before.

'Good morning,' the captain said as he poured himself a cup of coffee from the urn on the cart. 'These two seemingly unrelated deaths are too alike to be a coincidence. I have assigned my most brilliant detective and my best M.E. to solving these mysteries.

'You will each report to your respective supervisors, and they in turn will report to me. Doctor Cannon was unable to attend this morning, so Lieutenant Baker will fill him in.'

The captain, Lieutenant Baker, Jamie and Sam spent the next two hours becoming completely familiar with the known facts about what one scandal rag reporter called 'the bleeding eye deaths'.

'Mr. 'R.R.' is a good storyteller, but not

much of an investigative reporter,' the captain told them. 'He seems to be very knowledgeable about urban myths. He's been writing his load of manure for over twenty years. He'd love to turn this into a new version of *The Rocky Horror Picture Show*. Be very careful what you say around him. If we've discussed all that we currently know, then Lieutenant Baker and I have departments to run.'

The captain and Lieutenant Baker left the room, and Jamie and Sam remained seated, each feeling as if they had just been given the third degree.

'How did R.R. know about the broken blood vessels in the eyes?' Sam wondered.

'There are always leaks,' Jamie told him. 'There is an orderly that I understand is currently looking for a new employer. I think that was where R.R. got his information.'

'What would you like to do to him if we find another case like this one and he finds out?'

'Strap him to a chair, fill him to the gills with an old-fashioned truth serum, and make him tell us where he gets his information! Or maybe just start shooting off his toes until he begs me to let him tell all that he knows!' Jamie declared.

Sam laughed. 'Do you really think that would work?'

'Not really,' she replied. 'But it's a fun fantasy.'

2

'What?' Jamie was incredulous. 'Why would you think that louse could be trusted as a snitch? He's a self-serving, lying, no-good, slithering snake in the grass who's been railroaded out of at least three tell-all tabloids like the *Midnight Confessor!*'

'Because we know exactly what he is,' Sam answered her, 'and that he will always think of himself first! That, and his knowledge of urban legends, makes him the perfect person to find out what we want to know. We are both agreed that our victims must have been killed with an as-yet-unknown, possibly experimental, weapon that leaves no tell-tale sign of its usage.'

'Except for broken blood vessels in the eyes,' Jamie interrupted.

'Do we still have the bodies?' Sam asked. 'Have any family or friends come forward to claim the remains?'

'No,' Jamie replied, her anger starting

to cool slightly. 'Why do you ask?'

'I think perhaps we need to check the head area again. See if there is the tiniest mark that can't be explained on either, or both, of the bodies.'

'But I checked the bodies thoroughly!' Jamie insisted. 'I even opened the skull and looked for bruises to the brain tissue! There *weren't* any anomalies to be found.'

'I want to see for myself,' was all Sam would say. 'I still think we'll find something.'

'You're insufferable!' said a frustrated Jamie.

'If I'm right, I'll buy you dinner at Johanna's just to gloat!' Sam teased.

'And what happens if there's nothing to be found?' Jamie wanted to know.

'Then I'll still buy you dinner, and add Johanna's famous ice cream sundae as your reward.'

⋆ ⋆ ⋆

Later, in the morgue, Jamie had the two bodies laid out on examination tables.

While she prepared to reopen the skulls to check the brain tissue, Sam probed the hairline near the temple of the first victim.

'What's this tiny reddish mark near the ocular orbit?' Sam wondered aloud.

'What mark?' Jamie asked, stepping up beside him.

She peered at the almost invisible mark that Sam had indicated. 'Could be a birthmark or some other blemish.'

'It appears on the other side, too! Let's check the other body to see if it's got the same marks!'

'Why not? I missed this the first time.'

They checked the other body, and found the same tiny reddish marks at almost the same exact spots.

'Now we have an anomaly to work with,' Jamie said. 'Only I don't have any idea what it means!'

'Check and see if there are any signs of broken capillaries in the brain tissue underneath the mark,' Sam suggested. 'Some sort of energy source may have passed through the skin and into the brain.'

'Being so near the eyes, with all of their blood vessels, it probably didn't stop until it hit the other side of the skull. I'll check in a straight line from one side to the other.'

* * *

Two hours later, Jamie and Sam were cleaning up.

'Want to shake down a slimeball tomorrow night?' Sam asked Jamie as they toweled their hands dry.

'I told you that I don't want to have anything to do with that lying piece of illegitimacy! What does he know that we could possibly want from him?' Jamie's face showed her distaste for the idea.

'Just a theory.' Sam rubbed his face in a weary gesture. 'If there are any rumors about a government cover-up of a new weapon, he's the man who has heard them. Besides, don't you want to play 'this little piggy' with him? You can use your weapon to count.'

'Cops aren't allowed to use that type of

interrogation method, and you know it!'
Jamie retorted.

'No,' Sam agreed, 'but we can do 'bad
cop, worse cop' and make him think we
would really love to hurt him. We want
him so scared he won't worry about
protecting his sources. You get to be the
'worse cop' and have all of the fun.'

'That almost makes being in the same
room with R.R. worthwhile,' Jamie sighed
wearily.

★　★　★

'You don't have to like snitches,' Sam was
telling Jamie. 'You just need to be willing
to use them as information sources, just
like Google.'

'At least Google doesn't turn my guts
inside out!' Jamie said. 'And also, Google
wouldn't try to quiz me back, or get drool
all over me like a dog eyeing a juicy
bone!'

'Oh.' Sam was beginning to understand. 'So you've been interviewed by our
favorite cesspool reporter! Then he will
believe you when you tell him you want

to remove his toes without anesthesia. He already knows that I'd just as soon break his face as spend any quality time with him.'

'Let's just get this over and done.' Jamie shuddered. 'Then I can go home to a nice hot bubble bath!'

'There he is now!'

R.R. walked into Johanna's and swaggered over to the bar.

'Set me up with your thickest steak and your best bottled beer,' he ordered, placing a fifty-dollar bill on the counter. 'I just got paid for that story about the super-Taser that was stolen from the military's new weapons supply house. I'll bet that's what done in them two over by the hardware store and the milliner's.'

Sam and Jamie looked across their table at each other as they listened to R.R.'s boasting.

'I got the straight goods on this one,' he said as he gulped his beer. 'This super-Taser is use of deadly force. Not some bleeding heart stun gun. Get hit with this one up close and personal, you're singin' with the angels.'

14

'You were right about the rat knowing where all of the trash is buried,' Jamie whispered across the table. 'He's put me in the mood for some 'this little piggy'!'

'Just remember, we want him able to talk,' Sam replied, 'not drugged-out on painkillers.'

'Well, let's just say that he won't be thinking of me as a sex object anymore. Look, he's leaving.'

'We'll catch up to him at the alley, where we can talk privately.'

Jamie and Sam followed R.R. outside minutes later. As they saw him heading up the street to his apartment house, a man in dark clothing, who looked like he could tangle with a Mack truck and come out the winner, stepped away from a light pole, lifted R.R. off of his feet, and slammed him against the building.

'You mouth off anymore about the super-Taser,' a surprisingly high-pitched voice uttered, 'and you won't be singin' with the angels, 'cause your mouth will be filled with your cement coffin.'

Mixed with the man's size and

strength, the voice was unusually intimidating.

'I think you may want to let that man go,' Sam said mildly as he and Jamie came closer. 'He might give you a disease!'

'Stay outta this, pretty boy!' the man squeaked. 'You and the girl got no business here.'

'Now, that tears it!' Jamie spat at him. 'He's calling *me* a girl, when he's going to need my expertise with a scalpel to remove my foot from his backside!'

'*Pretty boy*, indeed! He's going to need dental implants and a nose job if I get to him first, Doctor Watson,' Sam added. 'After all, this man is our collar, not his.'

'What do you mean, 'your collar'?' R.R. gasped. 'Who *are* all of you, and what do you want with me?'

'I'm your worst nightmare!' said Squeaky-voice.

'Bad cliché,' Sam responded. 'Besides, you are in error. I'm *your* worst nightmare, and she's your *worst nightmare's* worst nightmare! Now, stand down and let that man go, or die to regret it.'

'Huh?' whimpered R.R. 'Isn't that 'live to regret it'?'

'Naw,' Jamie grinned. 'He'll wish he hadn't lived that long.'

The big man said coldly, 'Enough chit-chat!' Then he dropped R.R. and charged the couple facing him.

Less than ten seconds later, Squeaky-voice was on the ground, out cold, and bound hand and foot.

'Is he dead?' R.R. couldn't believe what had just happened. 'What did you hit him with? I was thinking the super-Taser was a hoax!'

'He's alive,' Sam responded.

'That was simply a little-known Eastern self-defense move,' Jamie added. 'We just hit from both sides.'

Sam called for a uniformed unit to pick up the big, squeaky-voiced man.

'Do you want to press charges? We already have him for assault on a police officer,' he asked after he disconnected.

'Are you kidding?' R.R. exclaimed strongly. 'He'll come looking to make ground meat outta me when he gets bail! You two gonna be able to watch over me twenty-four-seven? *I don't think so!'*

'If you play nice,' Jamie replied with a malicious grin, 'and tell us everything you know, have heard, or even suspect about this super-Taser, we could maybe be in a position to make him and his friends go away.'

'All right!' R.R. said exasperatedly. 'You keep him on ice until the next issue of the *Midnight Confessor* comes out on Tuesday, then meet me on the south side of the monkey pit at the zoo that afternoon at three. I'll answer all of your remaining questions then.'

3

'What do you think about this super-Taser?' Lieutenant Baker wanted to know from Sam and Jamie after they had processed Squeaky-voice into a cell. 'Is it for real?'

'We don't know, Lieutenant.' Sam tried to get comfortable in his chair. 'The *Midnight Confessor* is supposed to have an article about it in next Tuesday's edition, according to R.R.'

'He's promised to fill in the blanks,' Jamie said as she leaned back in her chair, 'if we can make Squeaky-voice and his friends go away, and not bother him until after Tuesday's paper hits the news stands.'

'That's liable to be not quite doable,' Lieutenant Baker told them. 'It seems that his friends have lots of money, and they can make the mayor and the commissioner roll over and play dead whenever they tell them to. Tiptoe around these guys if you must, but the captain wants these cases solved. Do we have any new leads that might give us a connection between the two dead men?'

Sam checked his notes. 'All that I've been able to find out is that one was traveling on business from the east coast somewhere, and the other was on vacation from the dot-com business, Lieutenant.

'The businessman made his living investing in produce futures. The vacationer owned several industrial farms. That could be a link that I'm working on.'

'It's a tenuous link at best,' the lieutenant agreed. 'However, it's the best lead that we have. Check Google, Facebook, Twitter and YouTube, and see what you can find out about them.'

'Another thing that we believe we know,' added Jamie, 'is that they were both killed by some sort of electrical or sonic wave capable of bursting blood vessels and possibly sending any vital organs in its pathway into a state of deadly paralysis. I think that's what caused the deaths.'

'Okay.' Lieutenant Baker waved them out the door in dismissal. 'See what else you can find out about our two victims. And then pump R.R. for everything he thinks he knows.'

★ ★ ★

Sam and Jamie were at his desk in the squad room and they had started checking all of the personal information websites for any connection between the two men.

'I often wonder how my great-grandfather would have made use of all of our modern technology,' Sam mused as they checked to see if they had any hits from their computer search. 'According to my grandfather, he did amazingly well solving crimes in nineteenth-century Europe that baffled his contemporaries; using logic, astute observations, and a highly specialized knowledge of many field related to criminology and human nature. My great-grandfather's best friend chronicled several of their adventures together in his journals.'

'Did your great-grandfather's friend have a colleague who became a well-known author?' Jamie asked. 'Are they by any chance related to the famous nineteenth-century detective team who was believed to be the creation of an imaginative medical-practitioner-turned-writer?'

'My great-grandparents came to this country when Grandfather was a baby to avoid the coming war with the Axis powers. I joined the force here hoping to avoid that connection and make my own reputation as a detective.' Sam was seemingly embarrassed. 'Too many people were inclined to make a big deal of the family name. I thought of using my great-grandmother's maiden name, but in recent years her diaries were found, and her name, exploits, and connection to her famous husband have become too well-known.'

'My great-great-grandfather seemed to have avoided that kind of notoriety,' Jamie said. 'He shared his journals with a colleague who turned them into the seemingly fictitious tales that many believed that they were. But weren't they supposed to be contemporaries?'

'According to Great-Grandmother and family history, she met Sherlock Holmes after he had retired to raise bees and write several monographs on his studies. My great-grandmother, who was a precocious orphan in her mid-teens when they met, was not impressed at their first meeting. At that time, she had little respect for his 'declining' abilities. Seeing her potential, he convinced her to become his protégé and apprentice.

'Years later, they realized that their mutual respect for one another had grown into love. Despite the large gap in their ages, they had a long and happy relationship.'

'Well, I suppose we each could have been paired with less gifted — and less intriguing — partners,' was Jamie's response.

'And I think that more regular assignments would probably border on the dull side for both of us.' Sam grinned. 'At least, that's been the case for me so far.'

4

The internet search soon revealed that, while the two men had apparently never met, their business interests had been slightly interconnected. The futures broker had invested heavily in the types of produce that the farming industrialists provided.

'Both men seem to have inherited a sizeable portion of their wealth at a very young age, which they each had parlayed into businesses worth many times what they had started with,' Sam remarked as he studied the electronic pages on the screen.

'Can we extrapolate yet a reason why these two were in our city and why they might have been singled out?' Jamie pondered. 'Can we rule out random chance?'

'Random chance is a possibility,' Sam answered, 'but with a very low probability. My question is what these two young entrepreneurs could have done to have brought this kind of deadly attention upon themselves. What was their hidden relationship?'

The hour was getting late and their minds were getting fatigued. Sam and Jamie both decided to go home and return on the morrow, hopefully refreshed and with new approaches to their problem.

Sam arrived the next day to find Jamie waiting for him.

'Are you willing to accompany me to the morgue?' Jamie said in greeting. 'It seems that a new death came in this morning that we need to investigate.'

'What have we got?' Sam inquired as he accompanied her to the morgue downstairs.

'The deceased, a young female, seems to have been our young broker's personal assistant and public relations person.'

'Any similarities between her death and the other two?' Sam asked.

'Her body was found in the same general area of the city, and she does not appear to have been robbed or molested in any way,' Jamie replied as they reached the doors to the morgue's prep room. 'One difference was that the deceased had an expression of terror on her face. I think she may have seen her assailant and knew what was about to happen.'

Jamie and Sam put on scrubs in preparation for the autopsy. They entered the examination theater and approached the body of a young woman, about thirty years of age, and of average height and weight with dark brown hair.

Sam stood back out of the way as Jamie began her examination and report.

After recording the time and known facts about the deceased, Jamie began with her observations of the body's visible markings and physical state.

'The deceased appears to have been in a highly agitated state at the time of death,' she began. 'Facial features show evidence of fear — or possibly disbelief — of her upcoming fate.'

Jamie removed the sheet covering the body. 'No sign of wounds or other physical violence. No signs that the deceased struggled with an assailant; no evidence of skin or blood under the fingernails has been found from the preliminary examinations.'

'What's this?' Jamie peered closely at a small reddish mark between the breasts of the body on the table. 'The deceased exhibits a tiny mark at the center of her chest resembling an electrical burn.'

'Do you think we'll find the kind of damage to the blood vessels in the chest area that we saw in the eyes of the other two victims?' Sam wondered; quietly, so as not to cause the voice-activated recorder to react to him.

Jamie's only response was to prepare to open the body's chest.

'There appears to be massive trauma to the heart muscle and the aorta,' she said into the recorder. 'There appear to be no wounds to the chest cavity or the heart, but several blood vessels, as well as the aorta, appear to have burst, causing the heart to go into paralytic shock and possibly for the vessels to bleed themselves out.'

Jamie continued to give the body a thorough examination, taking tissue and fluid samples for the toxicology lab, and reporting all of her observations into the recording.

'I think we may be seeing a more powerful example of this new electrical gun,' Sam said as they finished up in the morgue. 'This time, the weapon did not appear to have been placed against the victim's skin, and yet the internal trauma caused was sufficient enough to have caused death very quickly.'

'I tend to agree with your conclusions, Sam.' Jamie was trying to make sense of her findings. 'Except for the fact that the woman was an employee of the broker, and the possible electrical burns, there doesn't seem to be any direct connection between the three deaths.'

'I'm going to research recent conventions that might have brought our three victims together,' Sam said as he approached his desk. 'They all chose to come to London, California for a reason.'

The search turned up negative for local conventions, so Sam expanded his search to include nearby communities. When that also came up negative, he tried events at the Indian casinos in the area.

'Bingo!' he cried. 'All three were booked into the nearest Indian casino's hotel two weeks before the first victim was found. Now, what were they doing here in London? Shopping perhaps?'

'Or maybe having a clandestine meeting with their killer for the purchase of the weapon? Could they have been the victims of a deal gone bad?' Jamie replied.

'Let's see what R.R. has to tell us tomorrow after the issue of the *Midnight Confessor* comes out. We may possibly find out something interesting.'

The next day, just as soon as all of the papers were placed on the news stands, Jamie and Sam were looking for the article by R.R.

'Something's wrong,' Jamie, frustrated, told Sam. 'There *is* no article with R.R.'s byline, nor is there any word on a missing secret weapon.'

'Let's arrive at the monkey pit before three and see if R.R. shows up.' Sam was not taking this calmly. 'If he does, we grill him and find out what happened to his story, and get him to give us what he knows — or else.'

'Or else, what?'

'We turn him over to Squeaky-voice.'

'Sounds like a plan to me.'

★ ★ ★

At the monkey pit, Sam and Jamie watched the visitors come and go. Since it was relatively early on a weekday, it was easy to spot R.R. when he showed up, looking over his shoulder and trying, unsuccessfully, not to be obvious.

As they fell into step with him, Sam said quietly, 'What happened, R.R.? Did you and your editor get cold feet?'

R.R. jumped visibly. 'You scared me almost outta my shoes! It wasn't my fault that the piece didn't run!'

'So give with the excuses, and don't forget to grovel!' Jamie told him.

'Some guys came to the offices and started flashing badges and gettin' real pushy with my editor. They said that they were gonna shut the paper down if we printed the story. Claimed they were some sorta federal agents and it was a matter of national security.'

'You sure you're telling us the truth, R.R.?' Jamie said with menace. 'Which flavor of alphabet soup did they claim to be connected to?'

'I don't know!' R.R. claimed plaintively. 'They never said and I didn't see their badges. They flashed 'em real quick to the boss, and he didn't argue with them very much.'

'How were they dressed?' Sam didn't like what he was hearing.

'Dark blazers, cheap ties, grey dress pants, and black loafers with thick rubber soles.' R.R. shrugged. 'Real generic stuff. Oh, yeah, and powder-blue dress shirts with button-down collars.'

'Sounds like fakes to me, Jamie,' Sam told her. 'Even the city pays enough to their plainclothes officers for a decent suit!'

'Now that your editor has caved in to these bozos,' Jamie glared as she spoke to R.R., 'how are you going to bargain for protection from that squeaky-voiced giant? He's going to make bail soon if we can't give the judge something serious, like a history of felony extortion convictions. We need some high-powered evidence to keep him locked up until the trial.'

R.R. went pale, and started explaining what he had heard from an informant of his who worked inside the army's weapons development department.

'The new weapon is just a souped-up version of the hand-held stunner that used to be sold over the counter for self-protection — before the kids got to playin' around, tryin' to see who could take the longest jolt without passing out. This one is supposedly strong enough to kill if used for more'n a second or two. I couldn't get information on that. Then, three, maybe four, weeks ago, this guy tells me about a big flap over at the new weapons holding area. It seems that two working prototypes turned up missing when they did a surprise inventory.'

'Any idea how close you need to be when you use this weapon?' Sam looked R.R. straight in the eye. 'Does it have to be touching the skin, or can you put some distance between you and your target?'

'My contact didn't say,' R.R. claimed, 'and I don't think he knows. He's a pretty low-level worker. He assembles parts in the manufacturing department. Most of what I got from him was hearsay on the line.'

'I'm beginning to believe that this is more than just simple hearsay,' Jamie responded. 'Too many people are involved in this super-Taser thing.'

After advising R.R. to find a hole and pull it in after himself, Sam and Jamie returned to the station. As they sat in the break room discussing their conversation with R.R. at the monkey pit, Lieutenant Baker walked in.

'Well,' he began as he grabbed a cup of coffee from the pot on the counter, 'we've identified Squeaky-voice. His real name is 'Big John' Akker. He's been arrested for using strong-arm tactics half a dozen times, but with no convictions. He got into a fight once and put a guy into the hospital for three weeks. John got ninety days for aggravated assault and battery. We can hold him without bail on the 'assaulting police officers' charge as a flight risk, but if the judge doesn't agree before the case goes to trial, he'll have a good chance to make bail.'

'That doesn't sound good for R.R.,' Jamie told him. Then she and Sam told the lieutenant about the events at the *Midnight Confessor*'s office that had caused the story to be pulled before it went to press.

'The guys that rousted the editor didn't sound like your typical government agents,' Sam said. 'They sounded like a couple of toughs trying to look like government types. They may have even been ex-cops.'

'Well,' Lieutenant Baker said as he finished his coffee and stood up, 'we'll try to hold Big John for as long as we can. His lawyer is working real hard to get the judge to set bail, and the D.A.'s office is trying just as hard to convince the judge that Big John is a flight risk.'

Jamie and Sam prepared their reports together in the break room, comparing notes, before going to their respective desks to type them up and print them out to hand over to Lieutenant Baker and Doctor Cannon. When they were done, they decided to stop at Johanna's for an early supper and to relax before going home to their separate homes.

As they walked in, they were greeted by several patrons calling out good-naturedly such enquiries as, 'Have you solved the 'Case of the Missing Heir', Sergeant Holmes?' and 'Found any clues to the 'Adventure of the Severed Ear', Doctor Watson?'

'Pay them no mind,' Johanna told them as she led them to a quiet booth. 'They've put your names together with the famous detective duo of the nineteenth century. Now that you've been officially teamed up together, everyone's kinda proprietary toward you. Sorta like rubbin' shoulders with celebrities.'

'Not that we don't appreciate it,' Jamie and Sam commented together, 'but it would help our present investigations if they weren't quite so voluminous, Johanna. It's almost embarrassing!'

'I'll pass the word among the staff,' Johanna replied with a smile. 'Most of the patrons'll follow their lead if they see you being treated no different than themselves.'

'Thanks,' Sam gratefully told her for himself and Jamie. 'We both enjoy your hospitality. This has always been a good place to relax.'

5

The following morning, early, Sam and Jamie went to the Army weapons factory north of the city limits. They were shown into the office of a lieutenant colonel and waited for him to finish a phone conversation in an interconnecting office.

'Thank you for waiting,' he said as he entered the room. 'I'm Lieutenant Colonel Rembrandt, officer in charge of this factory.'

He held out his hand to each of them. 'What can I do for you today?'

After everyone was reseated, Sam and Jamie showed Lieutenant Colonel Rembrandt their badges.

'I'm Detective Sergeant Holmes and this is my partner, Doctor Jamesina Watson, M.E . . . '

'You're not really serious, are you?' Rembrandt laughed. 'I thought Holmes and Watson went out with Basil Rathbone and Nigel Bruce!'

Seeing the look on the faces of his guests, the colonel felt chagrined.

'We are *very* serious, Colonel,' Jamie replied indignantly, 'as someone with a name like yours should be! These are our true names, and we have three deaths that we believe may be related to rumors of a security breach here at your facility about a month ago.

'These deaths appear to have been caused by what we believe to have been a new and powerful version of the electrical stun gun sold over the counter a decade or two in the past,' Sam continued, 'which may have gone missing from your inventory three or four weeks ago.'

'The development and disposition of all pre-issued weapons is classified.' Colonel Rembrandt's face went cold as he replied. 'I'm not at liberty to comment further. This interview is at an end. Please do not seek to interrogate any of our civilian or military personnel. The corporal will escort you to your vehicle and see that you leave the parking lot. Good day.'

On the way back toward downtown,

Sam remarked, 'I have the feeling we may have just been given unofficial confirmation of R.R.'s information.'

'That's what the bum's rush was all about?' Jamie talked as she drove. 'I thought that he just didn't like our multi-generational relationship to the Great Detective and his friend.'

'Yeah,' Sam replied, looking out of the window. 'I didn't care for his opening remarks, either.'

As they entered city traffic, Sam's eye caught a familiar figure walking away from them.

'Jamie, isn't that our friendly squeaky-voiced giant walking down the sidewalk on the right?' Sam was upset that Big John had already made bail. 'His lawyer must have used up plenty of favors.'

'Yeah,' Jamie answered. 'He just turned left onto Jane Avenue! Shall we tail him?'

'It could be interesting to see who he joins up with, couldn't it?' Sam said thoughtfully. 'There's a parking garage about a block from where he turned. If he goes in there, let me out and then find a space.'

Just as Jamie turned onto Jane Avenue, she saw a tall man matching Big John's description go into the parking garage. Pulling into the driveway, she slowed down just enough to let Sam out and for him to keep an eye on their suspect. The big man approached the stairs and headed down toward the basement parking area.

Using his cellphone, Sam sent a text message to Jamie and let her know where he was. Big John was met near the elevator by two average-sized men in cheap suits. Both men looked as if they could have been from the Mediterranean area near the Middle Eastern states.

'What have you found out about that reporter?' the first man asked Big John. 'Does he know that we have the weapons?'

'I learned nothing,' Big John answered in his high, squeaky voice. 'When I started to question him, a man and a woman interrupted us. When I tried to scare them away, they hit me with something and knocked me out. The next thing I knew, I was being held without bail for assaulting police officers.'

'How is that you are here, then?' the second man asked menacingly.

'My lawyer finally convinced the judge that I wasn't no flight risk. Then my boss found a bail bondsman to pay my bail. What do you want me to do now?'

'Find the reporter, and make sure that he hasn't revealed what he knows. We'll take care of the editor and his paper,' the first man said in a voice as cold as a glacier.

The vibration alert on Sam's cellphone buzzed him. Jamie's text alerted him that she was about a hundred feet away from him on the other side of the suspect group. Pulling out his weapon and his badge, Sam held them out as he stepped out of the shadows.

'Freeze!' he yelled. 'Police officers! Place your weapons on the floor and your hands on top of your heads, and get down on your knees!'

'Do as he says!' Jamie yelled from the other side. '*Now!*'

'You led them to us!' the second man spat as he pulled out a device that resembled a large cellphone. 'Die, betrayer!'

The man placed the device less that an inch from Big John's throat. There was a buzzing noise, made loud by the hollow-sounding echoes. The big man twitched violently for the moment or two that the object was aimed at him. Both Sam and Jamie fired their weapons at the man who had shot his super-Taser.

The other man fired a similar weapon in Sam's general direction, and then dodged behind a stretched Lexus. Sam ducked down just as something hit the wall behind him. He saw a spot in the plaster about the size of a quarter begin to glow for a moment — right where his head would have been — and turn to powder explosively.

By the time he recovered, he saw Jamie dodge out of the way of the speeding Lexus.

'Call it in,' Sam shouted over his shoulder as he ran up the stairs. He hoped that he could get back up to the street level in time to get a better description of the Lexus: possibly get a partial license plate number.

He reached the street level just in time to see the taillights as they vanished, heading to the right, and melded into the traffic.

'Dammit!' was all he could think to say.

6

The uniformed units had arrived quickly, with the officers from Internal Affairs following a few minutes later. While Sam and Jamie were giving the details of events leading to the shooting, the paramedics were able to stabilize the man who had been hit twice by the shots that were fired at him.

'Okay,' the older of the two detectives, a grey-haired black policewoman with twenty years on the force, was saying, 'tell us again the events that led up to you firing your weapons. Sergeant Holmes, we'll take you first, and then we'll talk to Doctor Watson.'

Sam explained how their evidence search had led them to the army's weapon development and manufacturing center, and that the officer in charge had told them that any information about missing weapons, experimental or otherwise, was classified, and had had them escorted off of the property.

'Then, on the way back to the station,' he continued his report, 'I saw a man — who we had arrested for assault on police officers after witnessing him roughing up a citizen that we wished to interview — walking on the sidewalk. My partner and I decided to follow him. At that time, we only wished to learn more information about his activities and his contacts.

'We followed our person of interest into this parking garage. I got out and followed him downstairs while Doctor Watson found a parking space for our car.

'Our man met with two others, wearing nearly identical inexpensive suits with striped ties and black wingtip loafers. Both of these men spoke English that was lightly accented, and they appeared to me as if they could have been from the Mediterranean or Middle Eastern areas.

'As I eavesdropped on their conversation, I was led to believe that they meant to do harm to a certain reporter who had given us information that his paper was supposed to have printed yesterday. The story was withdrawn before being published after two men claiming to be government officials of some sort had made noises about national security.

'Doctor Watson had just texted me that she was in position, so I identified the two of us as police officers and ordered them to lay down any weapons that they had and to surrender. The man closest to Big John, our person of interest, pulled out what appeared to be a large Taser type of weapon and fired it at our man's throat. He twitched violently and fell to the floor. As the weapon that we felt had been used in three deaths seemed to have the properties of a super-Taser, we felt that our lives were in danger and we both fired our weapons, striking the man who had used the Taser weapon.

'The other man fired what appeared to be a similar weapon in my direction. I dodged just in time to avoid being hit, and the shot struck the wall behind me. The plaster exploded outward from the wall in a small explosion.'

Jamie was questioned, and she gave the same report to Internal Affairs, only from her own point of view.

'What evidence did you have for believing the reporter about the super-Taser, Doctor Watson?' Detective Shirley Brooks, the veteran detective, asked.

'The only marks on the outer skin of the three victims were reminiscent of electrical burns,' Jamie responded confidently, 'and all three showed signs of trauma to the capillaries and other blood vessels in the path of the possible shockwave.

'When our reluctant informant described the weapon, it sounded plausible with what we knew of the unknown weapon's abilities.

'The weapons used against us here this afternoon were most likely used in the other deaths. What we saw of the super-Taser's capabilities tells me that it is much more dangerous than we at first were given to believe.'

'Sergeant Holmes — ' Detective Brooks turned her attention back to Sam. ' — please show Detective Ronston the area where the weapon's shot hit the wall. Doctor Watson, let's take a look at the dead man. I want to see this mark you spoke of, if it's there.'

The dent in the wall at head-height was possibly an eighth of an inch deep and in the shape of a slightly irregular circle.

'The plaster from the wall seemed to explode away from the point of impact, much the same way that a ricocheting bullet might have done. I would say that wall was less than fifteen feet from where the shooter was when he fired at me. The other man fired his weapon from about an inch from Big John's throat. Big John had been hit for less than a second by the time Doctor Watson and I realized what was happening and fired our weapons. Remember, neither of us had encountered a weapon like this before, and our reactions may have been slowed down as a result, Lieutenant.'

Pictures had already been taken of the floor where Big John lay, and now the photographer took pictures of the wall while the distance from it to the body was measured. This was found to be about twelve feet.

'Big John appeared to have been hit in

the throat,' Jamie told Detective Brooks. 'We should find a mark somewhere between the chin and the clavicle areas.'

Jamie lifted the big man's chin, and then loosened his high collar.

'Yes,' Jamie told Brooks as she pointed to a small raspberry-shaped mark. 'This is the mark that I found on the other victims. And look here at the edge of his shirt collar. See the scorch marks?'

'I do,' Shirley Brooks commented. 'How do you think the second weapon was able to fire a blast to the distance of twelve feet with enough power to gouge the plaster? Taser weapons that don't require skin contact have to fire wire-guided leads that carry the stun charge to the target and close a contact switch to knock someone down.'

'Maybe,' Jamie surmised, 'the development of wireless technology allows a contact dart to be activated remotely once the dart makes contact with the target. Otherwise, the device acts like a normal hand-held Taser, but with a deadly amount of amperes added to the voltage between the contact leads.'

'Okay. Doctor Watson, Sergeant Holmes.' Detective Brooks put away her notebook. 'Unless something is revealed between now and the time our report is finished, you should be off paid administrative leave in a day or two. The standard rules of engagement for officer-involved shootings seem to give you two a justified one.'

The forensics and Internal Affairs teams released the scene to the ambulance operators, who took Big John's body to the morgue. Everyone else got into their vehicles and returned to the station. Jamie and Sam slowly walked to their car as the adrenalin rush from their fight-or-flight experience began to wear off.

'What do you want to do now, Sam?' Jamie asked as she unlocked the car doors. 'We seem to be at loose ends until the report clears us to go back on duty.'

'Normally, I'd go home, nuke a TV dinner and enjoy a novel by Asimov, or Heinlein. Somebody like that. Or maybe a Hillerman book,' was Sam's response.

'A real bookworm, eh?' Jamie was intrigued. 'I always have preferred reading to watching television when I wanted to relax.' Sam was a little wistful. 'What do you do to relax?'

'It depends on my mood.' Jamie smiled. 'If the weather is nice, I go for a walk or a bike ride. Other times, I just putter around the apartment with my journal or drawings.'

'Times like this,' Sam sighed heavily, 'I'll go drown my sorrows in a big gooey chocolate dessert. You care to join me?'

'Johanna's has the best chocolate anywhere!' Jamie grinned mischievously. 'And the atmosphere is great for what ails us, too.' Sam laughed, his spirits already starting to lift.

7

Johanna's was just starting to get busy with the early-dinner crowd when Sam and Jamie arrived. Johanna personally showed them to their quiet booth in the corner near the back wall.

'Everyone's heard about what happened at the parking garage on Jane Avenue,' she explained as she set down two pots of hot herbal tea. 'Can't keep secrets in a cop bar. I thought you might need a pick-me-up. I know that neither of you use alcohol, so how 'bout my decadent chocolate crème de menthe sundae instead?'

'That's the best offer I've had all day!' Jamie replied enthusiastically.

'Make that two,' Sam added.

★   ★   ★

'You know,' Sam said a short time later, 'Johanna's doesn't have the atmosphere of a cop bar, the way they did in LA. This almost has the feel of a nice family restaurant.'

'Remember how Johanna did her best to make us feel comfortable with the jokes the first time we came in here after we were first partnered up together?' Jamie asked. 'She knew that we would want to be accepted for what we could do as a team for the department, and not become worried about being put in the same mold as Sherlock Holmes and Doctor John Watson, so she got the staff to get the teasing down to something that we could live with.'

'Yeah,' Sam said thoughtfully. 'And she's made us fit in by having our own table for when we need to discuss case problems privately, without being disturbed. She seems to do that for most of the detectives and uniformed officers. She's very good at getting the best out of everybody on the force.'

Jamie and Sam watched the crowd of regulars as they enjoyed the ambience of the bar and grill. Not all of the customers were current or retired police officers, they noticed. There were a large number of reporters and families out for a relaxing night on the town.

About midnight, Jamie took Sam back to the station's parking lot so that he could pick up his own vehicle and drive home. They said their goodnights, and Sam walked to his car as Jamie pulled out onto the street. As he unlocked his door, he heard the sound of a powerful engine and the screeching of rubber. He looked toward the sound and saw a stretched Lexus coming at him at a high rate of speed.

Jumping out of the way, Sam did his best to get a license plate number. He was sure that it was the same vehicle that had been driven away from the scene at the Jane Avenue parking garage earlier that afternoon. The Lexus swerved to the left at the last moment, barely missing Sam and his car. He heard a buzz and the rattle of banged metal.

As the Lexus sped out of the parking lot, Sam reached for his cellphone and speed-dialed the night dispatcher.

Sam gave the dispatcher the details and

the location of the attack. Soon the police band was buzzing with the news of the attack and police units on the street were alerted to the vehicle's description and the partial license number that Sam was able to get.

Within minutes, officers who had been at their desks were out in the parking lot, checking for any other signs of unauthorized personnel. While Sam was giving his report on what happened, Jamie's car raced back into the station's parking lot.

'I heard the dispatch call.' Jamie's voice quaked with concern as she came to a stop near Sam. 'Are you all right?'

'Yes,' Sam replied. 'The other man we had our run-in with this afternoon came back for another try. I got out of the way when he tried to run me down, and then I think he fired that super-Taser at my car. The driver's door took the hit. It looks like a small hammer was taken to it. I think this thing must have an adjustable power source.'

'The lab has the other super-Taser and is going to be giving it a thorough examination,' the night watch lieutenant told him. 'Your car will need to be impounded while we check everything out. I'm sorry, but it's now part of a crime scene. We'll get you a temporary replacement within the hour. As soon as it arrives and your report is finished, you can go on home. I'd advise you to get some rest, if you can. This attack corroborates your story, so it looks as if you and Doctor Watson should be off paid administrative leave by the end of today.'

'I'll meet you in front of the library at nine,' Jamie told Sam. 'You bring the coffee and donuts, and we'll do some research on the development of the Taser.'

'Bring your laptop, too,' Sam advised. 'I think we should look into the database on arms dealers while we wait for the library to open. These guys seem to want this weapon for some heavy-duty purpose. They'll stop at nothing to protect their investment. I'm beginning to think that this is our connection between all of our victims.'

Sam's replacement car arrived a few minutes after he had finished answering questions and filling out his report. He accepted the keys and drove himself home.

In the morning Sam drove his car into the library parking lot. Jamie arrived two minutes later. They got out of their cars and went over to a picnic table and checked out the police database on known arms dealers.

'Too bad that we don't have access to the government database,' Jamie sighed. 'I bet that we could find our man if we did.'

'Well, I think we just got a break.' Sam was excited by something they had found. 'Look at the man just barely in the shot here.'

'That's Big John!' Jamie exclaimed. 'Who are these people in the group shot?'

'The caption with the picture says that they belong to a consortium of businessmen from several different groups known to buy, steal, and sell arms to anyone with enough funds to make it worth their while. Our man in the hospital is the third from the right. The one next to him is the one who tried to run me down last night.'

'Okay,' Jamie said as the library doors

were unlocked. 'Let's see what the library computers have on the history of the Taser gun.'

They entered the now open library, found a couple of unused terminals, and began their research. Twenty minutes later, they found out that the Taser had been developed originally as a non-lethal means for subduing violent persons without putting the officer on the spot in harm's way. The inventor had been a fan of the old Tom Swift novels and he had named his invention the 'Thomas A. Swift Electric Rifle', which gave the new weapon the acronym of 'TASER'. The files that Sam and Jamie found gave the history of successes and failures of the use of the Taser in law enforcement. It was found that often people under the influence of PCP and other drugs were unaffected by the level of stun provided by the electrodes allowed in use.

Jamie's laptop signaled that she had an incoming e-mail. When she opened her e-mail server, she saw a message from Doctor Cannon.

'We just lost our best lead,' she told

Sam. 'The guy from the parking garage died without regaining consciousness. Doctor Cannon also says that early DNA reports a possible very close relationship between our first two victims.'

'That doesn't agree with the identification found with the bodies.' Sam was puzzled. 'It's beginning to look more like an arms deal gone bad. I think that we need to look a bit more closely at Messrs. Gilden and Mason.'

Just then, Sam's cellphone vibrated. 'Detective Sergeant Holmes,' he answered. After listening for a few moments, Sam told the person at the other end of the connection that he and Jamie would arrive in twenty minutes.

'Get the print-out on the Taser and meet me in the station's Conference Room A,' he told Jamie. 'Lieutenant Baker says that Lieutenant Colonel Rembrandt and an FBI agent named Jones wish to talk to us about our case.'

'I hope they don't want to take this away from us,' Jamie said dryly.

They got the print-outs from the printer at circulation desk after logging off at the library's computer. They went outside to where they had parked their cars. Fifteen minutes later, they walked into the conference room together.

After introductions were made and everyone had shaken hands, Special Agent in Charge Jones opened the conference.

'Normally,' Jones began, 'the FBI would take the lead in a case where three government agents were killed while setting up a sting operation. However, this case also involves the theft of an important weapons development and the plans for its eventual mass military production.'

'After 9/11,' Colonel Rembrandt added, 'this information could undermine the public's confidence in our ability to protect the average citizen.'

'The government has issued the two of you a very special security clearance,' Lieutenant Baker continued. 'These gentlemen believe that since you're already so deeply involved, you're in the unique position to plug the leaks in their weapons development and help to break up this group of international racketeers.'

'Who were the two men identified as Gilden and Mason?' asked Jamie. 'The information we got from their identification indicates that they didn't know each other. The early DNA reports say that they were too closely related for that to be likely.'

'They were both deep undercover agents for a special task force. They were first cousins living in separate areas of the country since their recruitments. Their cover legends were that they laundered money used to buy black market weapons for resale to various groups inside and outside the country. This allowed them to infiltrate some of the groups that had acquired weapons caches that we wished to keep here at home.

'Apparently, they got found out and were eliminated, along with Gilden's secretary, Ms. Amagon.'

'When you came into my office at the weapons plant asking about the super-Taser,' Colonel Rembrandt said, 'I couldn't be sure that you weren't with this latest group calling themselves the

'Golden BBs'. Our reports told us that they deal exclusively in hand weapons of extremely versatile and deadly potential. Weapons such as the super-Taser were exactly what they dealt in. Militia and terrorist groups both would like to have these kinds of weapons. A weapon as silent and deadly as the super-Taser could be used to cause panic among the law-abiding public, as well as being the perfect weapon for assassination. Used by gangs, the lack of traceability would be a godsend.'

Jamie and Sam silently agreed with this train of thought.

'What, exactly,' Lieutenant Baker asked, 'do you wish my people to do? Two of their suspects have died and their informant has gone into hiding and his associates have been harassed by men posing as government agents.'

'We want them to continue their investigations into the deaths of our sleeper agents and into the thefts of the super-Tasers,' Agent Jones replied. 'We'll be investigating how the leaks were passed to your informant, and do what we can at our end. Lieutenant Baker, I would like you and Doctor Cannon to coordinate Sergeant Holmes' and Doctor Watson's reports with my office. The lieutenant colonel and I will keep you up to date on our findings.'

Special Agent in Charge Jones and Lieutenant Colonel Rembrandt picked up all but one of their folders, placed them in their briefcases, and prepared to leave the room.

'This folder contains all of the information known about the Golden BBs, including everything that can be found on the internet,' Jones told them. 'Hopefully, its contents will lead you to new conclusions. The conclusions of our own analyses will be sent to you in three days, giving you time to form your own opinions.'

'We would like to have the results, along with your conclusions, which you have reached through your own independent investigations at that time,' added Rembrandt.

Picking up their briefcases, the two left Lieutenant Baker, Sam, and Jamie sitting at the table, looking at one another. Getting up from the table and heaving a sigh, Lieutenant Baker left without further comment.

'I guess that means we're being left on our own.' Sam wasn't very pleased. 'We'll get the blame if we fail to stop these people, and hopefully, a pat on the back if we bring the top echelon to justice.'

'This sounds like something your great-granduncle would have dreamed up for your great-grandfather,' Jamie commented.

'According to Grandfather, his uncle's assignments were even more clandestine after his father had teamed up with his mother,' Sam continued. 'Several members of the Diogenes Club were agents for British intelligence under my great-granduncle before, and after, the Great War. Of course, by the time Great-grandfather and Great-grandmother had begun working together, he routinely used them all over the world in his information gathering network. In spite of Great-grandfather's unusually good health, Great-grandmother increasingly felt that her brother-in-law was uncaring for the welfare of his younger brother and his sister-in-law, using them in the most dangerous assignments with almost no information given about what they were supposed to be looking for.'

'Let's hope that we are as successful as they were,' Jamie sighed with resignation.

8

Sam and Jamie met in one of the community conference rooms of the library as soon as it opened the next day. They had spread out the contents of the folder that had been left by SAC Jones and Lieutenant Colonel Rembrandt on the table, along with their own reports, print-outs, and notes.

As they went through everything in front of them, they made a list of all of the different bits of information that had been collected about the Golden BBs, their past operations, and everything that the police labs had gotten from the captured super-Taser before having to turn it back to the military. The file that had been given to them gave a little more information on the weapon, but not much, and nothing that they were allowed to share with their colleagues.

'Your theory about how the weapon may have used wireless technology to deliver the shock to the targeted victim from a distance seems fairly close to the fact,' Sam remarked as they collated the information from the different sources. 'The super-Taser fires a splinter-sized dart that penetrates the victim's clothing, making contact with the skin; then the shooter presses a button, and the dart delivers a high-voltage, high-ampere, electrical shock.'

'What it did to your car door proves how, if one is in contact with an electrical conductor, just how deadly its potential is — even with a near-miss,' Jamie opined. 'You could have been killed if you had been touching your car when it hit the door.'

'I don't even want to think about it!' Sam said uneasily. 'I think we need to have that heart-to-heart with R.R. that keeps getting sidetracked.'

'I agree,' Jamie grimaced, 'but he still makes my skin crawl.'

'Let's park your car at your place, go looking for him, and pay him a long-overdue visit after we're done here.' Sam was already putting the information into related groups. 'We'll know then what types of questions we need to ask. He may not want to talk to us after what happened to Big John, but I think we can convince him that it would be easier to protect that hide of his that he holds so dear if he talks to us now, rather that later.'

Sam and Jamie worked on organizing their information for another hour and a half, before heading to the station to put everything into a protected and encrypted file on the computer on Sam's desk and a copy onto Jamie's laptop.

'Next month's personal budget's gonna include one o' those,' Sam said longingly. 'Yours is proving to be a very useful item.'

'Having a wireless internet connection is what made me think of how the super-Taser might be used without wires,' Jamie said. 'After all, signals for cell and cordless phones also use electronic radio-type waves that way.'

'Chalk another one up for Thomas Alva Edison,' was Sam's comment.

★   ★   ★

Jamie and Sam finished transferring their notes to their computers and then went to the conference room to discuss the questions that they wanted to ask R.R. The time was approaching the rush hour, and they figured that R.R. would probably be starting to feel relaxed by the time that they caught up with him at one of his hang-outs.

'Johanna's is the highest-class grill and bar that R.R. can afford,' Sam told Jamie, 'and he doesn't go there unless he just picked up a bonus for a story. Normally, the places that he frequents can only be called 'dives'. Most of them are real dumps. If a place we want to check out is more than you're able to handle, just let me know. I'll go in and look for him while you wait in the car. If I see him, I'll try to talk him into coming outside to meet with us. Otherwise, we can make sure we convince him to get into the car with us after he comes out. Okay?'

'No,' Jamie said neutrally, 'I think I'll be safer going in with you. These people need to see us together sooner or later, now that we've been made partners. It might just as well be now.'

'Okay, then.' Sam wasn't sure that he agreed. 'Just follow my lead when we go into these places, and remember — the offer still holds if you feel you need to change your mind.'

Sam explained that their search would begin at one of the better of R.R.'s habitual places.

'He'll probably go to one of them first,' Sam was telling Jamie as they approached the parking lot of Chuck's Deli and Diner, a hangout for reporters looking for possible scoops on their rivals. Joe's Eatery was where they would look next if they didn't find R.R., or any information as to where he might be located.

Sam pulled his department loaner into Chuck's parking lot and found a space. As he got out of the car, he told Jamie, 'Most of the print newsies stop here, or at Joe's, when they're trying to find something newsworthy. Then they start looking in the less-established neighborhoods. The locals are always looking to score a few bucks by selling information.'

'And the lower the class of neighborhood, the more anxious they are to sell?' asked Jamie.

'Right,' Sam answered, 'but the information isn't always as reliable as the better places. You have to get to know who you're dealing with. You need to be able to sort out your sources. After a while, you get a sense as to when your source's information is worth listening to. If it *is* worth listening to, and the price agrees with your assessment, then you are wise to pay for it. Normally, if the informant refuses to budge very much from his asking price, it's fairly reliable.'

They walked into Chuck's and found a table in a quiet corner where they could watch most of the clientele. The waiter approached them and they both ordered teas.

When the waiter returned with their tea, Sam asked, 'Have you seen R.R. today? He said that he might have something to give me.'

'He owe ya money?' the waiter wanted to know.

'Not exactly,' Sam stalled. 'More like a trade.'

'He hasn't showed up here for a couple o' days,' the waiter informed them. 'You want me to give him a message if I see him?'

'Just let him know,' Sam replied after a moment's thought, 'that the big guy with the squeaky voice isn't gonna be looking for him anymore. And tell him that Holmes and Watson are looking for the bad guy that took him outta the picture. We'll make it worth his while to get in touch.'

Sam left a twenty dollar tip on the table and paid for the tea at the cash register when they left.

'Why did you leave such a big tip?' Jamie wondered as they got back into their car.

'So that he would remember to give R.R. the message,' Sam informed her. 'After his run-in with Big John, and the rousting he and his boss got at the news office, R.R. may be keeping below the radar. Let's try Joe's next.'

★　★　★

After getting the same results at Joe's that they had gotten at Chuck's, and leaving the same message, Sam decided to try a lot lower down on R.R.'s list of dives.

'If he's trying to hide, he may decide that his friends and informants around here may be more likely to protect their source of income,' Sam theorized. 'The trouble with that line of reasoning is that these low-lifes are just as likely to sell him out if the price is right. I've even known some of them to turn in their own family members. I'm hoping that we can catch up to him before someone from the Golden BBs does.'

Sam and Jamie drove over to the east side of the city, where the natural underground lake that gave London, California its water supply, and that had created its desert oasis, was located. This far toward the city limits, the houses tended to be rundown adobe huts and wooden shacks built before 1900, and cheap housing put up during the Depression era following the 1929 stock market crash. The houses were often homes to drifters and squatters.

Rosita's Cantina had never seen any good days. It had started as a roadhouse during the Prohibition era, and had never gotten any better. Even the alcohol had never been of a quality much above bathtub gin and bootleg beer.

'If R.R. is hiding here,' Jamie observed, 'he must believe that his situation is really desperate.'

'Yeah,' Sam agreed. 'I guess he's hoping the camouflage can keep him alive. I wonder what he knows that makes him so fearful.'

'Or maybe what's happened,' Jamie said. 'Something sure has him running scared. You said that he doesn't come out to the desert area unless he really needs something.'

'Do you want to go in with me,' Sam looked at her as asked the question, 'or do you want to stay in the car with the doors locked?'

Before Jamie could answer, the front door of Rosita's blew off of its hinges, and flames could be seen through the opening. Jamie speed-dialed 911, while Sam grabbed the fire extinguisher from under the dash and ran to the door.

He reached the open doorway and began to spray a path through the fire with the flame retardant in a desperate effort to aid the victims inside. He could see several people on the floor. Some were already to rise and flee the building.

Sam kept spraying at the flames in the front area near the door and the bar. Seeing the cantina's fire hose, he grabbed it and began a fresh assault on the fire. He was succeeding in lessening the spread of the flames as those less injured began to control their panic enough to aid their more injured fellow patrons to safety.

Fortunately, there were only about a dozen persons at Rosita's that night. The explosion appeared to have been confined to the areas near the front door and at that end of the bar. The shockwave had mostly traveled through the front doors, and the fire had spread quickly across the exit — and would have blocked any escape if Sam had not been as quick as he had been with his fire extinguisher.

Jamie had begun to help evacuate the

injured and to set up a triage area by the time the fire and rescue crews had arrived. Her efforts had been assisted by several of the people, and because of everyone's efforts, there had been only one fatality.

The bartender had apparently been returning a bottle of whiskey to the shelf when a spark seemed to cause it to explode into flame, causing a very large and hot sympathetic explosion behind the bar.

The fire was quickly doused and everyone received treatments for various burns, cuts, bruises, and some relatively minor injuries. The police and fire investigators questioned everyone who was able to talk to them and could give them answers.

'You and Doctor Watson seemed to have been at the right place at the right time,' the fire investigator said to Sam after he had been examined for possible burns and smoke inhalation. 'What were you doing so far from your home district?'

'We were hoping to find a print

reporter that may have had some information about a case we were working on,' Sam replied noncommittally. 'This was believed to be a place that he frequented occasionally.'

'Okay,' the investigator continued, 'tell me what happened from the time you arrived until the explosion and fire.'

Sam told the investigator that they had just arrived at the parking lot and were starting to exit their car when the front door was blown outward off of its hinges by a fiery explosion.

'I grabbed the fire extinguisher from the car and started working on the flames at the front exit,' he reported calmly. 'Doctor Watson called 911, reported what had happened, and requested assistance at this location.

'I kept the flames away from the door as best I could, so that the patrons inside had a chance to escape. When my fire extinguisher was running low, I spotted the fire hose and began to use it to douse the flames. Doctor Watson began to triage those that needed medical assistance until the emergency units arrived.

'The bartender appears to have been at the site of the explosion. I found him badly burned, as if the shelves of liquor bottles had suddenly burst into flame.'

★ ★ ★

After his interview with the fire inspector, Sam went looking for Jamie. As he searched, he saw an EMT applying burn cream to a face that was very familiar, despite its crosshatching of minor cuts that had already received touches of mercurochrome or merthiolate.

The EMT finished his ministrations and allowed the police to question his patient.

'Hello, R.R.,' Sam said as he walked over. 'Close call in there tonight.' Then he turned to R.R.'s interrogators and showed them his badge and ID. 'I'm Detective Sergeant Samuel Holmes, LPD, homicide division. Mind if I sit in? I came here hoping to find R.R. before something happened to him.'

'You were the one who kept the flames away from the door?' a young uniformed officer wearing corporal's stripes on his sleeve questioned.

'Yeah,' Sam told him.

The corporal held out his hand. 'You took a real chance in there, but you saved several lives.'

Sam took the offered hand as the other officer, wearing the tribal police uniform of a nearby band of Amerindians, spoke up in a deep voice.

'A couple of the tribal elders were in that cantina looking for one of our younger members.' He also held out his hand. 'The tribe owes you a debt of honor for what you and Doctor Watson did here tonight. You'll be welcome whenever you stop at the chapter house.'

The corporal began to question R.R. about what he had heard and seen when the fire exploded inside the building.

'Where were you sitting, sir?' he inquired of R.R. after getting his name, address, and occupation. 'Did you see or hear anything that could have been related to what happened?'

'I was sitting at the bar, about three stools away from the door,' R.R. began.

'The bartender had just poured a couple o' drinks for the waitress to take to one of the tables. The waitress put the drinks on her tray and went to deliver them. The bartender was just putting the bottle back on the shelf when it seemed to flare up like a torch and several other liquor bottles all went off like a Forth o' July celebration. I was knocked outta my seat and onto the floor.

'When I was able to get up off o' the floor, I saw that someone was keeping the flames away from the door. Several people were headin' for the exit, some of 'em was trying to help their buddies or girlfriends. I saw a kid, who looked barely legal for bein' in here, lying spread-eagled on the floor by an overturned table. An old guy, whose coat had been scorched, was tryin' ta get him up and movin'. I dragged myself over and helped the old man pick up his young friend and we got outta there.'

'Did you hear a buzzing sound?' Sam was intrigued by the sequence of events. 'Did you see a spark when the bottle broke?'

'Would it matter,' the Amerindian officer asked, 'how the whiskey ignited? What if the bartender was just unlucky enough to have set the bottle down hard enough to break it and cause a spark at the same time? Couldn't it just be an unfortunate coincidence?'

'Not if a super-Taser was used!' R.R. was suddenly worried. 'Sergeant, I did hear a buzzing sound, sorta like the sound a noisy cicada makes, just before the bottle exploded in the bartender's hand. I wasn't sure until you said somethin' just now.'

'Did you know that Big John, the squeaky-voiced giant who tried to rough you up last week, was killed?' Sam asked him. 'He was talking to some friends in a parking garage when Doctor Watson and I showed up.'

He described the subsequent fatal battle, and the later attempt on his life in the police parking lot.

'The forensics people figure that if I had been touching my car,' he concluded, 'I wouldn't be talking to you right now.'

9

R.R. promised Sam that he would meet him and Jamie at the zoo's monkey pit the afternoon of the day after the fire. He also promised to bring all of the notes he had made during his investigations into the super-Taser.

'I want to make sure that that thing is never pointed my way,' he croaked out of his dry throat. 'By the way, thanks for keepin' the fire from the door long enough for all of us to escape. There were some close friends and associates of mine in that bar tonight. I've picked up some of my best stories from them over the years. You know, the type that made my boss happy and paid me well.'

By the time Sam dropped Jamie off at her apartment house, it was two in the morning. Sam walked with her to her door, keeping a sharp lookout for a stretched Lexus or anyone watching them.

'Keep your doors locked tight tonight,' he told her. 'The Taser guy may have been in Rosita's earlier. I think he took a shot at R.R. and missed. He hit the liquor bottle instead, and accidentally started that fire. He was probably near the rear exit and figured that no one would make it out.

'If he hung around long enough somewhere nearby, he may know that his intended victim escaped, and that we were there in time to help save everyone but the bartender.'

'I'm wondering,' Jamie's face had a thoughtful look, 'if he truly realizes just how deadly that weapon really is. Look at the devastation the super-Taser has caused just from near-misses.'

'Definitely a weapon of mass destruction if used by the wrong people,' Sam commented.

Jamie entered her apartment. When Sam heard the locks engage, he cautiously went back to his department loaner. As he unlocked his car door, he heard a car engine roar to life and the squeal of tires heading in his direction. He quickly dove

for the pavement as far away from anything metallic as possible. A dark-colored
luxury SUV sped by, and ordinary bullets
were fired from a backseat window.

As the SUV sped out of sight, Jamie
came rushing out of her apartment,
weapon in hand.

'Holmes!' she yelled. 'Are you all right?'

Sam picked himself up off of the
sidewalk, dusted himself off, and said,
'I'm okay, but they killed my car. Being a
street cop was never *this* dangerous.'

'Do you think that the department will
take the replacement cost for losing the
second car in two days out of your pay?'
Jamie joked nervously.

'Gee,' Sam replied with a groan, 'I hope
not! I haven't bought this paycheck's
groceries or paid this month's utilities
yet!'

Sam and Jamie waited with nervous
relief for the patrol units to arrive.

★　★　★

'Well,' Lieutenant Baker scowled at Sam
as he read the report about the drive-by

84

shooting of the department's loaner vehicle, 'at least the door to your personal vehicle has been replaced and CSI has finished looking it over. How did you attract such deadly attention to yourself? Didn't this start as a nice, quiet homicide investigation?'

'The trouble is, Lieutenant,' Jamie said in Sam's defense, 'it always seems to get more complicated as Sam and I look deeper into these mysterious deaths. It's become more like peeling an onion. The more layers that are removed, the more involved we find ourselves.'

'First of all,' Sam interjected, 'we started with two seemingly unrelated deaths. Then a closer examination showed not only the broken blood vessels in the eyes that we had seen before, but that both of the victims also showed small, reddish blotches at the temples near the hairline. Then, a day or two later, a third victim was found. She was soon identified as the previous victims' personal assistant. When Jamie examined the deceased, a similar mark was found over the breastbone. Underneath, the blood vessels in the heart, including the aorta, were also found to have been violently ruptured.

'Later, Jamie and I overheard a tabloid reporter bragging about a story that he'd uncovered. He was accosted on his way home by a man who told him to clam up about the 'super-Taser'.

'The next time we saw this big man, he was meeting with two other men our illustrious reporter had described as having caused his editor to pull the plug on the story for 'National Security' reasons.

'When the two men appeared to be threatening the big man, Jamie and I stepped in, announcing ourselves as police officers. The two men pulled out weapons and fired. These weapons, we now know to be the same ones stolen from the local military armory weapons development post. Our big man was shot at close range by one of the men and killed. Jamie and I returned fire, hitting the first shooter. The second shooter fired his weapon at me, just missing, and hit the wall behind me.

'As I recovered from avoiding his shot, the suspect got into a stretched Lexus and drove toward the street level. I attempted to get to the exit in time to get a license plate number, but I got there just as the Lexus turned onto the street and drove away.

'After Jamie and I had made our reports, she dropped me off at the station's parking lot to get my car. I was attacked by someone driving a stretched Lexus attempting to run me down. I got out of his path and he turned around to come at me again.

'As he drove by, I heard a snap and a sizzling buzz, just before the loud metallic crunch of my car door being caved in. This time, I was able to get a partial license plate number. I used my cellphone's speed-dial and called the dispatcher to tell them what had happened.

'Tonight, after a long day of checking facts on this 'super-Taser', we went to Rosita's Cantina, looking for our informant. When we arrived, the place explosively burst into flame. Afterwards, I dropped Jamie off at her apartment. When she had gone inside, the lights of a dark-colored SUV came on and it sped toward me.

'I dove to the pavement and avoided both the car's frame and the bullets fired from an automatic weapon. Having heard the gunfire and squealing tires, Jamie dashed out of her apartment, her weapon in one hand and her cellphone held to her ear with the other. Neither of us had a chance to get a good description of the SUV or its license number.'

'One thing's clear.' Lieutenant Baker pulled at his ear. 'The captain is getting whatever he was looking for when he teamed you two together.'

10

The horse-faced man with the Mediterranean complexion stared at his subordinate. His face was flushed with anger as he attempted to control his emotions.

'Three times you have failed to remove this insignificant and meddlesome detective,' Horse-face finally screamed, spittle spraying the other man's face. 'This level of incompetence will not be tolerated! Bring me news of his death, and that of his partner, within two weeks or you will find yourself taking a long, cold nap in their city morgue. Oh, and don't forget to take care of that reporter and the traitor who sold him the information.

'Now, get out there and don't come back until you have done your job. We meet with our client in ten days, and I don't want to have any loose ends lying around to trip us up.'

Pale-faced and obviously shaken, the thin, hatchet-faced subordinate with the noble nose and acne-scarred cheeks swallowed the hard lump in his throat as he nodded his head in acknowledgement of his orders, and then backed out of the office. As he closed the door behind him, he heard his boss's phone ring.

'This had better be good news,' the boss growled into the receiver. He listened a moment before adding, with a malicious smile on his face, 'Alright. Leave him in the lobby of the newspaper office with a note saying 'traitor' pinned to him.'

The horse-faced boss had a look of satisfaction on his face as he replaced the receiver back on its hook.

★ ★ ★

When the office secretary checked the lobby of the *Midnight Confessor* and saw the man, she let out a piercing scream of fear.

The person sitting in the chair was badly beaten, and had been cut in several places. A bloody trail led from the sidewalk, through the door, and to the chair in which he had been deposited. The trail appeared to have been left as if the body had been dragged in off of the street through its own blood.

The secretary's scream had brought the editor and several reporters running into the lobby. One of the reporters put his hand over his mouth and ran for the nearest receptacle in which to empty his stomach. The editor sent everyone back to their desks and dialed 911.

'A badly beaten man has been left in the lobby of the Midnight Confessor,' he told the operator. 'Please send paramedics and the police to 9591 Circle Three Drive. The man may still be alive, but I don't know.'

The editor went back to the reporters' floor and attempted to calm his people down. Spying the most stable reporter, he said, 'Johnson, wait outside on the sidewalk and lead the emergency units to the victim. Keep everyone away from the building. Everyone else is to stay out of the way. They'll come in here when they're ready to get details. You are all reporters, so just report the facts.'

The wait wasn't long before emergency sirens were heard. The editor went into the lobby, his balding head shiny with perspiration.

The paramedics and MD came through the door first. After a swift examination, the man was pronounced dead. The lead investigator had a quick conversation with the doctor and the paramedics, and then walked over to the editor.

'Who found the body, Mr . . . ?' he said in an even tone.

'Simon. I'm the editor,' was the returned answer. 'It was Ms. Juno, the secretary. She came out to check the lobby and found the body just as you see it. She's pretty upset.'

'We'll get this over as quickly as we can, sir,' the investigator told him as Sam and Jamie walked in.

'Hey, Lex,' Sam greeted the lead investigator with a warm handshake. 'Are you in charge?'

'Yes, I am,' Lex answered. He looked over at Jamie and asked, 'Who's your partner? I haven't seen you paired up with anyone since you worked the streets.'

'This is Doctor Watson, from the FME department,' Sam told him as Jamie held out her hand. 'We're working on a couple of cases that may have a connection.'

'Mind if I have a word with your medical team?' Jamie asked.

'If the docs don't mind,' Lex gave Jamie an appreciative look, 'neither do I.'

Jamie walked over to the body and the medical team and introduced herself. The doctor began showing her various points of medical interest.

Lex and Sam went to the reporters' room. There, Lex commandeered the editor's private office for his interviews. The secretary was called in first.

'Ms. Juno,' Lex began, and then introduced himself, 'I'm Detective Lex Willet, and this is Detective Sergeant Samuel Holmes. Would you please tell us, as best you can, what happened out front this morning? I know that the situation was traumatic, but we need to get down everything that happened while the events are still fresh in your mind.'

'I really don't know that I can be much help,' Ms Juno began, weeping. 'I was so terrified by seeing that bloody and bruised man, sitting in that chair when I looked out into the lobby, that nothing seems real.'

'What made you check the lobby at that time, Ms. Juno?' Lex asked next. 'Do you have a routine which you go by, or is it random?'

'Nothing like that,' was Ms. Juno's answer. 'Normally I'm sitting at my desk by the window, but I had just returned from the powder room, and looked out of the window as I took down the 'Back in 15 minutes' sign. That was when I saw him out there.'

'So, you didn't see or hear anything?

'No,' the secretary responded. 'The powder room and the reporters' room doors were both closed, and so was the lobby window.'

Sam asked, 'Did you see or hear anything from the lobby window before you left for the powder room?'

'I did see a car parked outside by the curb.' Ms. Juno had taken a moment to think before she answered. 'But since I didn't notice anything unusual about it before I closed up the counter, I didn't think anything about it. I didn't pay it any attention.'

'So,' Lex resumed, 'nothing attracted your attention until you returned and looked out of the lobby window?'

'That's right, Detective,' she responded. 'I don't think I'll ever forget that horrible sight!'

★ ★ ★

Lex and Sam interviewed all of the personnel at the *Midnight Confessor*'s office without getting much information. *Maybe*, Sam thought, *the medical examiners will have more luck with the body.* About all he could tell was that the body was that of a young male, perhaps thirty to thirty-five years of age, and that he had been tortured maliciously, with a cold expertise in prolonging the pain.

'What information could the perps have possibly wanted so badly that they would go to the lengths of using such a vicious and unnecessarily brutal method?' Lex wondered.

'It wasn't to get information, Detective,' Jamie said as she joined the two men. 'The perpetrator was sending a message. One that he enjoyed sending. He was given free creative rein to inflict as much pain as he could, for as long as he could, but with the stipulation that the victim would definitely die in the end.

'Our victim took several days to die. Several of the bruises had time to change color. Others are fresh. Also, I believe that the cuts were made in such a way and over enough time to allow the victim to bleed for several hours, if not a full day. This sick mind considers death by torture to be an art form.'

Sam looked at Jamie. During the week or so that they had been partnered, he had come to respect her ability to 'wear the skin' of a killer.

'Anything else, Doctor Watson?' Detective Willet wasn't sure what to think of the pretty FME. 'Do you expect to find anything new during the autopsy?'

'Possible signs of strangulation that was halted just before death, then resumption of the other tortures. At a guess right now, he was beaten, cut, then strangled — in rotation. The only signs of torture that I've haven't seen yet have been burns. He'll have to be completely laid out at the morgue. Some evidence may be hidden by the wrappings on the body.'

The forensic team had finished with their pictures and measurements, and okayed the victim's placement into a body bag and his removal by the paramedics for transport to the morgue. Jamie and the MD rode away in the ambulance.

'She got all of that, just by a visual examination?' asked Detective Lex Willet.

'She's the fifth generation of Watsons in the field,' Sam explained. 'You might say that her great-great-grandfather and his detective friend invented many of the techniques being used today.'

With a satisfied grin hidden behind a hand, Sam watched as the other detective's jaw dropped.

11

The hotel suite was full of the aroma of the just-delivered meal. The slender, horse-faced man in the expensive slacks and dress shirt checked the uncovered dishes, and with a satisfied smile, handed the waiter from room service a large tip, signed the check, and dismissed him. The heavy-boned man with the hatchet face and acne-scarred cheeks sat on the sofa with a hungry and envious look as he watched his boss open his napkin and begin to eat.

'The traitor was dropped off as you ordered,' the man began. 'The lawmen arrived quickly and sealed off the block. Within half an hour, the body was removed and the evidence people were set to work corroborating the interviews and evidence. Our man watched for an hour and a half before the place was allowed to become normal again.'

'And our targets?' Horse-face asked.

'Did our agent see any of them?'

'Only the detective and the doctor,' was the reply. 'The doctor went with the medical group when the body was taken away, presumably to the morgue. The detective was among the last to leave. The whereabouts of the reporter is unknown at this time.'

The boss's face became a frightening mask and his cold gray eyes took on the hue of gun metal.

'I want that reporter found, and made to tell us what he knows and what he has passed on to these upstart detectives. And then I want him to disappear. Not a trace, understood?'

The other man's hatchet face paled as he nodded his acknowledgement of his orders. Then, having recognized that he was dismissed, he got up from the sofa and left his boss to his meal.

★　★　★

After the room-service cart had been removed, the horse-faced man took out his cell-phone and dialed a memorized number.

'The message has been delivered. We'll meet at the prearranged site for a demonstration at the sixteenth hour in ten days.'

'Very good, Clark,' the voice at the other end replied. 'Take care of the meddlers by then, or the deal is off.'

Clark switched off his phone, put on his blazer, and walked out of the door. In his blazer's pocket was an odd-looking pistol.

The hotel was equipped with an old-fashioned elevator operator, and she greeted Clark with a smile.

'Going out for a while, Mr. Stephanos?' she inquired as he got on the elevator.

'Yes, Julie.' Clark smiled pleasantly. 'I don't think that I'll be back by suppertime. Please inform room service that I'll be dining out this evening.'

Julie pushed the button to go to the lobby floor as soon as the doors closed.

'I'll do that, Mr. Stephanos,' she said as Clark Stephanos dropped a five-dollar bill into her tips jar. 'Thank you. Thank you *very* much.'

When the elevator stopped, Clark walked across the lobby to the street exit. The doorman blew his whistle for a taxi.

'Where to today?' he asked his hotel's most prominent guest as the cab pulled in next to the curb.

'Tenth Street and Queen Anne's Avenue, Jonathan,' he replied.

Jonathan opened the door of the luxury taxi that was part of the King's Hotel service, and gave the driver his fare's destination.

'Have a nice evening, sir,' he said as he closed the door.

Mr. Stephanos rolled down the window and handed Jonathan a thick envelope.

'Happy Anniversary.' He smiled at Jonathan's surprised look. 'The manager told me that tomorrow's your tenth year with the hotel. Take your family out for a night on the town.'

The window slid shut, and the driver eased into traffic as his fare leaned back into his seat and closed his eyes.

★　★　★

The taxi parked next to the curb in front of an antique book store on Queen Anne Avenue.

'That will be twelve-fifty, Mr. Stephanos,' the driver told his fare as he exited the cab. 'Shall I come back for you later?'

'No,' Clark replied. 'I'm meeting a friend inside. He'll drop me back at the King's Hotel later. Thank you.'

Clark handed him a twenty-dollar bill. 'Keep the change.'

The book store was a bit upscale for this area of the city. Tiffany globed lamps and well-padded leather covered chairs were placed in convenient areas throughout the large building. Replicas of paintings by Old Masters hung on the front wall between the windows. The other walls were lined floor-to-ceiling with shelves of books, both rare and not-so-rare. In one corner stood a coffee bar serving espresso, lattes, frappes, flavored and unflavored coffee. The entire room had the atmosphere of a nineteenth-century British gentlemen's club reading room.

The outside of the building was made of well-polished faux-cedar wood, stained to look weathered, but lovingly cared for. A plaque on the outside wall next to the door read: 'The Victorian Reading Room. Established 1902.'

Clark walked in, looked around for a moment, and then walked over to where four chairs surrounded a low table.

Seated in two of the chairs were a couple of middle-aged men wearing expensive suits, their ties loosened about their throats, and two-hundred-dollar imported shoes. Their demeanor was that of relaxed waiting. On the table in front of them sat two cups of Virgin Irish coffee.

'Gentlemen,' Mr. Stephanos said as he approached the two waiting men. 'Shall we retire to a more private area?'

A waiter approached them and requested Mr. Stephanos' order.

'A hot Almond Roast,' Clark told the waiter. 'And please bring it to my private corner.'

All three men then moved to the seating area reserved for them, in a cubicle made of sound-absorbent material.

Once they were all seated, Clark began his meeting.

'The traitor has been dealt with, and he has delivered his message. The reporter has gone into hiding. He will be found soon and eliminated. The two detectives are still asking embarrassing questions, and do not seem to be the type to scare easily nor to be corrupted.

'I have spoken with our buyer and he is still willing to negotiate in ten days.'

'Do we still have the product?' the older of the two men asked. 'I thought it had been captured when 'Abel' was killed in that parking structure.'

'We still have the second weapon,' Mr. Stephanos said sharply. ''Cain' escaped and delivered it to my hotel. Of course, 'Cain' has been punished for failing to avenge his brother. 'Seth' has replaced him and will extract our vengeance for us.'

The waiter brought Clark his order of Almond Roast. As he set it down on the table, he asked if there was anything they needed. Receiving shakes of heads, he left the three of them to their meeting.

'Who are these interlopers,' the younger man inquired, 'and why have they been allowed to keep interfering in our business dealings?'

'They have proven to be both resourceful and lucky.' Clark's eyes held the coldness of an Arctic storm. '"Lemech' is on the hunt for the reporter who knows too much, while 'Seth' plans the elimination of the modern-day team of Holmes and Watson.'

'Those two names again?' The older man seethed with anger. 'They have plagued businessmen like us for nearly a hundred and forty years! We have never succeeded against either of these families, nor have we been able to corrupt either of them.'

'We now have our opportunity,' Clark remarked. 'It seems that these two are the last of the direct lines interested in their ancestors' work. Neither of them is married, nor do they have progeny.

'Watson does have surviving parents and an elder brother. The brother seems to have no interest in the family legacy. Professor Watson is far more interested in academia than in dealing with criminal intrigue. He is married and has an infant son. The son will eventually be under our control.

'Holmes is an only child with no known living relatives. A few bold strokes, and their legacy will be gone forever.'

The three men continued to talk and to plan, until the waiter returned with the dinner menus and asked if they would like to order now.

12

Sam and Jamie sat in the living room of her apartment looking over the notes they had made concerning the Golden BBs. Their only concrete information was the reports on the open website of the FBI files.

'Let's look at that photo again,' Sam suggested. 'I want to know those faces as well as I know my own. These people are some of the most vicious that I have ever heard of. The FBI and CIA files have linked their dealings to some of the most gruesome vengeance crimes on at least three continents, as the death of R.R.'s informant proves.'

'Look at this footnote, Sam.' Jamie suddenly pointed to the text at the bottom of the page with the group photograph that Sam had referenced earlier. 'It says here that the group may have had its historical roots in organizations such as the Black Hand, and other illegal groups throughout the US and Eurasia. They may have been connected to some of the early militant jihad groups.'

'But why do they call themselves the 'Golden BBs'?' Sam wondered. 'Is that a reference to the lucky shot that shouldn't have killed its target? We know that they specialize in small arms that are extremely deadly, and difficult to trace or to detect.'

'Or maybe it refers to death from an unexpected source,' Jamie responded. 'The original Taser wasn't designed to kill, only to immobilize.'

'According to these notes — ' Sam continued reading. ' — they have stolen, and then sold, several unusual, but extremely deadly, small arms. From accurate poison darts and their air guns, to rings with tiny sharp points coated with the deadliest of concoctions, so that the tiniest scratch was all that was necessary to assassinate a troublesome dignitary. They deal in the perfect assassins' tools.'

The information was so sparse that speculation was all that the two detectives had to go on. The only solid facts that they had were that the group was acting locally for the present, and that they apparently had a buyer in the vicinity of London, California.

'The attacks on the *Midnight Confessor* and its personnel seem to indicate that the Golden BBs are close to a sale and that they will not tolerate any interference,' Sam concluded.

'If this were the late eighteen-hundreds,' Jamie's voice sounded weary, 'we could search for a mysterious professor who was the 'Napoleon of Crime', and eventually take down his criminal empire.'

'Even so,' Sam replied with a tired yawn, 'it took Great-Grandfather years to build his case, and to catch the majority of the Professor's colleagues. The masterminds always shield themselves with a well-founded cloak of respectability. Some never pay for the crimes that they plot in their lifetimes.'

About midnight, Sam and Jamie decided that they had worked as long as they could that night. They seemed to be going in circles, always coming back to the same points.

'Tomorrow is the day that I usually call my brother, James, and catch up on all of little Jimmy's antics,' Jamie said with a large yawn.

''Little Jimmy'?' Sam was tired, but interested. He and Jamie had not spoken very much about their families. 'Who is he? My competition?'

'He's my two-year-old nephew,' she said with a smile. 'James and I grew up in a close-knit family. Mom and Dad moved back to Dover, on the coast of England, after he retired from the UCLA medical center. James is a professor of history at UNLV. His wife was an attorney's assistant before she had Jimmy. Now she's enjoying being a stay-at-home mom. She says that she may go back to school and get her law degree after Jimmy starts kindergarten.'

Sam heaved an envious sigh. 'My parents married late in life and I was an only child. Since they were each only children, I grew up without cousins my own age. Unless I get married and have a son, I'm the last of the legacy. No more Holmeses to carry on the family name and traditions.

'It seems that no matter how large, or small, the family since Great-Grandfather's time, there has always been at least one male of each generation to carry on the family name.'

'Somehow,' Jamie said, 'I see you having lots of sons and grandsons. The Holmes name just seems to be too important to recent history to go peaceably into oblivion.'

With that, they said their goodnights, and Sam walked out to the street to his waiting vehicle. Being very careful and looking closely at his surroundings, he got into his car, and drove home without incident and without anyone following him.

★ ★ ★

The next morning, Sam woke up thinking about what Jamie had said about her family. *What if the leaders of the Golden BBs know about her brother and his family?* he thought. *Would they use that against her somehow? Could they be ruthless enough to harm them to get at her?*

Sam hadn't slept well the night before, thinking about what could happen to Jamie's family if their enemies knew what she had told him and decided that they could get what they wanted if they threatened to harm to any, or all, of her family.

In the short time that he and Jamie had been partnered, Sam had developed a definite friendship toward her. Their shared heritage was a factor, he knew; but he had felt an affinity with her when he first spoke with her in the break room at the station. Partners each watched the other's back and worked as a team, even when they disagreed on methodology. He and Jamie were still smoothing out the rough edges, but the pair of them were beginning to complement each other's strengths.

★   ★   ★

Jamie looked forward to her weekly chat with her brother and his family. She thought about how she, her brother, and her nephew all had names, or nicknames, which were forms of 'James'. Her great-great-grandfather's first wife had affectionately called him by that name, and he had called his son by his second wife 'James', too. Was that a subconscious way of remembering a lost part of his life? Whatever the reason, the name was used often over the following generations.

When Professor James Watson answered the phone, he sounded harried, but excited.

'My grant for a study of nineteenth-century London came through this morning,' he blurted out as soon as he heard his sister's voice. 'We'll be taking little Jimmy to see Mom and Dad while we're there. They sounded thrilled that they would get to really know their grandson. We'll probably be gone for six months to a year. We're scheduled to leave on the *QE2* next week, and I was going to call you this evening and give you the news.'

'That's great!' Jamie was excited for

him. 'I'm a little envious, though. My new partner is a descendant of the great detective himself and it has gotten me thinking of Great-Great-Granddad and the cases that they solved together. I'd love to see some of the places where they were supposed to have had their adventures. I think that Sam would, too.'

'I've heard that 221B Baker Street was a completely fictional address in the Victorian era,' he commented dryly. 'That address on Baker Street didn't exist until sometime in the twentieth century.'

'I know that a lot of the names and places were fictional.' Jamie was not to have her enthusiasm doused so easily. 'But it would be fun to look over some of the ground where those stories were said to have taken place. And of course Scotland Yard is there. I wonder if Lestrade and Gregson were real, or if Great-Great-Granddad made them up, too.'

'Well,' James laughed, 'we'll be sure to email you lots of pictures and send you a bunch of postcards. Oops! I'd better go! Jimmy is trying to help Alicia pack, and of course he wants all of his favorite toys and games to make the trip, too.'

James and Jamie said their goodbyes. As Jamie hung up her phone, she hoped that her brother and his family would have an enjoyable, but uneventful, trip to England.

Mom and Dad will be thrilled to see little Jimmy, she thought. Jimmy hadn't been born yet when they moved to England. Of course, they had made a trip back to the States when he turned a year old, but a trip like that was expensive and couldn't be done all that often. Now they would have six months to a year to spoil their only grandchild.

Jamie looked at the clock. It was almost time to meet with Doctor Cannon for her update on the effects of the super-Taser. The only hard facts that she and Sam had uncovered were from the autopsies of the four victims, and from the near-misses of the attacks on Sam. There were also the assumptions from the fire at the old roadhouse at the city limits, but nothing concrete. Just how was the sliver activated after it was fired, and how were the voltage and amperage controlled? Would the answers give them some way to protect themselves? She and Sam desperately needed to find that answer.

13

On the west side of the city, where the old records building had once stood, R.R. was waiting. He had received an anonymous tip that he would have the chance to know the name of the group that wished to buy the super-Taser if he was at the Birdhouse Fountain that afternoon.

The sun was warm and the flocks of pigeons were eagerly waiting for passers-by to drop tidbits of food on the ground. R.R. had bought a bag of sunflower seeds, and casually tossed a few out to the birds as he sat on a concrete bench just off of the cobblestone walkway surrounding the fountain. He watched the people walk by with a curious eye on the seemingly chance meetings around him.

When he felt the press of a cold gun barrel against his side, he was sure that he had been set up.

'Don't do anything dumb,' a voice

beside and a little behind him calmly advised. 'Yer Uncle Sam sends his 'greetings'. Yuh've jist been drafted.' R.R. felt something being slipped into his shirt pocket. 'Wait five minutes, and then walk over to the Burger King at the corner of King George and Queen Anne. Find a table inside and follow the instructions in yer pocket.'

As inconspicuously as he had arrived, the man left. R.R. was tempted to look back for the face that belonged to the voice, but decided that he really didn't want to know. He waited the required five minutes and scattered his remaining sunflower seeds to the pigeons. The Burger King he'd been told to go to was only a five-block walk north of where he was.

It was a cloudless, late spring day, the kind of day that California had once been famous for. R.R. strolled nonchalantly to his destination.

Upon his arrival at the Burger King, R.R. entered, ordered and received a small beverage, and then sat down at an unoccupied table. Before reading the instruction paper he had been given, he used his cellphone to call his editor, Mr. Simon, to let him know where his trail had led him so far.

'See if you can get in touch with Detective Holmes or Doctor Watson. Give them these instructions I'm goin' to read off to you,' he informed his boss. 'I want someone to know where ta start lookin' for me if I disappear.'

'Okay,' Mr. Simon replied, 'the tape is rollin'.'

'Here goes.' R.R. began to read from the paper that had been placed in his pocket. ''A blond woman in a flowered halter top and blue Bermuda shorts will greet you with a kiss on the cheek. Act glad to see her. After ten minutes of polite conversation, leave with her in her car. She will take you to where you will talk with an informant about the 'John Brown Society'. If you are followed by anyone except Holmes and/or Watson, you won't like the place where you will be left. Share the information you receive only with them. The lives of Watson's brother and his family depend on her getting this information.''

R.R. sat stunned. 'Get that message to them, now,' he finally said. 'I don't know how long it'll be before I'm contacted, and I don't know how long Holmes and Watson will need to get here. After that, they'll have no more than ten minutes to find me. I think that they're supposed to wait and watch until after the meeting, and I don't like that. It's too much cloak-and-dagger stuff for my taste.'

Mr. Simon promised that he would take care of his part of the plan, pressed the 'off' button on his phone, then dialed the number on the card that Detective Sergeant Holmes had given him.

The phone at the other end of the call was answered after it rang three times.

'Detective Sergeant Holmes,' the voice said. 'How can I help you?'

'This is Mr. Simon at the *Midnight Confessor*,' the editor replied, relieved to have reached the detective in person. 'I just got a call from R.R. and he had an interesting tale to tell. He was extremely adamant that you should hear the instructions that he was given. I taped our conversation, and I think that you should hear it immediately.'

Mr. Simon punched the playback button on his tape machine. The message was easily understood over the phone lines. When the recording was done, Sam asked, 'How long ago did R.R. give you this message?'

'Less than a coupla minutes ago,' was the answer. 'I called you just as soon as I hung up and found your card.'

'Do me a favor,' Sam said briskly; 'call the station and have them give Doctor Watson the same message that you just gave me. Tell them to have her meet me at that Burger King. I'm heading there now.'

Sam started his car and headed west to King George and Queen Anne Avenues as Mr. Simon called the police station with Sam's message.

'There's no telling how long before R.R.'s informant makes contact,' he told the person taking and directing phone calls, 'that's why Detective Holmes had me relay the information. He's going to see if he can be there before they leave the parking lot. My reporter's life and those of Doctor Watson's family may depend on knowing where he's been taken.'

* * *

Doctor Watson's cellphone began to play 'Flight of the Bumblebee'. She pulled it out of her pocket, and saw that the caller ID was from the police station.

'Doctor Watson here,' she answered.

'Doctor Watson,' she heard a familiar voice say. 'This is Lieutenant Baker at headquarters. We have an urgent message for you to meet Sergeant Holmes right now at the Burger King on the intersection of King George and Queen Anne Avenues. The information to be gained may be important to the health of your brother and his family. Start moving now and I'll give you the full message on the way.'

Jamie hurried to her car and started driving to the western limits of the city. She had barely begun driving when her cellphone rang again. Using the hands-free mode, she answered and heard Lieutenant Baker's voice.

'Just listen to the recording of the call that came in just before I called you the first time,' he said firmly. 'This was not a crank call. It will explain everything.'

As Jamie listened, her face grew pale and she choked back a cry of fear. Three of the most important people in her life were being threatened practically on the eve of a very joyous event for them. She was not about to allow a bunch of low-lifes to take away the joy and excitement that was rightfully her brother's. He had worked hard to get to his position on the faculty at UNLV.

Jamie drove on autopilot as she went to meet Sam. She knew that he was already working to keep her brother and his family from harm, and she was grateful. Who were these people from the John Brown Society, and what were their goals? The only John Brown that came to her memory was a reference to a man who had something to do with some event in pre-Civil War days. She couldn't remember if he had something to do with pro-slavery or anti-slavery. She only remembered that he had been ruthless and murderous.

The underground lake that made the city of London, California such an oasis provided a variety of vegetation that wasn't usually seen in the desert, but Jamie wasn't looking at it now. Her mind was working overtime on finding a way of protecting her family. The houses and palm trees and lush grass lawns passed by in a blur. Very soon, she was nearing one of the older portions of the city. King George Avenue headed west to meet Queen Anne Avenue which ran north and south. There, on the northeast corner, was the Burger King.

As she drove into the parking lot, she saw Sam's car. Apparently, R.R. and his contact hadn't left yet. Jamie locked her car and walked over to Sam's vehicle.

Without looking at Jamie, Sam unlocked the passenger door and let her in. As she slid into the seat, R.R. came out of the restaurant accompanied by a mature and good-looking blond woman on his arm. She was dressed in the clothing that he had been told to look for, and did not have the appearance of a 'working girl'. She was only an inch or two shorter than R.R., and affected an air of familiarity with him.

As they approached an older-model sedan, she used an electronic key to unlock the doors. R.R. looked around as if he was appreciating his 'girlfriend's' car. He spotted the two detectives but gave no sign that he knew they were there.

'You played that very cool,' the blond said as they got into her car. 'Of course, I knew that at least one of the detectives that I wished to follow us had arrived. Why do you think that it took me so long to meet with you?'

'I wasn't sure that the message had gotten to them in time.' R.R. glanced in the side view mirror on his side. 'Do you believe that they won't know that you want them to follow you?'

'If you reacted the way my friends and I knew you would,' she said as they left the parking lot, 'they'll get the idea anyway when I don't even *try* to lose them. We need them to have the information for them and for you.'

'Why is it so important?' The reporter's

instincts were working on overtime. 'Surely the actions of a small-time survivalist group aren't that important?'

'Not them,' his companion remarked, 'but the group that wants to supply them, and others, with the super-Taser. If they can disrupt the system enough, it'll be like the Prohibition and gangster eras, but with even more violence and rampant criminal activities. Our nation has enough problems with the subversive and criminal elements as it stands now.'

'So that's what your friend meant when he said that I'd been drafted.' R.R. shook his head in disbelief.

14

As Sam played 'Follow the Leader' with the car ahead of him, he gave voice to his feelings. 'She wants us to follow her. She's taking no evasive tactics, and is deliberately making it easy to tail her. I'm not sure I like this.'

'I feel that we're being set up for something, and R.R. is being used as bait,' Jamie returned. 'That comment in his instructions about my brother is just a little *too* dramatic. Why would anyone be after him? He's just a university professor.'

'You, your brother and his family, and I all represent the current generation of effective teams of criminal investigators.' Sam was conscious of the intrigue being used. 'Every one of us has done our part at one time or another to stop the Moriartys of their day. We're the ones that have to be stopped or nullified if they are to succeed.'

'I guess the old saying *ya knew the job was dangerous when ya took it* applies to us, doesn't it?' Jamie replied. 'I hope we can stop them before they harm little Jimmy. He's just a happy, innocent toddler. He hasn't even had a chance to get involved in what we do.'

'It could be their best chance to eliminate our legacy,' Sam commented. 'After all, there's only the five of us, and we've only just begun our careers.'

The car they were following pulled into the parking lot of an abandoned warehouse and stopped. The driver and R.R. got out, showing that their hands were empty. R.R. slowly walked over to Sam and Jamie.

'The lady requests that you join us for a chat,' he said. 'She claims to have vital knowledge related to our mutual endeavors.'

With his message delivered, he turned back to follow his escort into the warehouse. Sam and Jamie looked at one another in surprise, shrugged, and followed R.R. inside.

The warehouse interior did not show

the same signs of abandonment as the outside. The lights came on automatically as everyone entered. The walls were lined with shelves of electronic equipment, clothing, books, audio/video discs of every variety, and even those for storing computer files. Forklifts were parked ready to load pallets of all sorts of products and machinery onto trucks that should have been waiting at the loading docks.

The lady led the three of them to an office in the left rear corner where a dark-complexioned man in an automated wheelchair waited for them.

'Welcome,' his husky voice greeted them. 'Lydia, please bring our guests some refreshments, and then you may wait outside.'

After giving them choices of beverages, Lydia left to fill their requests. When she returned, she set each person's drink on the table that was beside each chair, and left them with their host.

'After having brought you here under somewhat devious means,' he began, 'I'm sure you are all three anxious to know the reasons. First of all, my name is Hugo Langsman. I'm the director of a 'black ops' branch of one of the national criminal investigation bureaus. We know that you have been asked by the FBI and Army intelligence to stop the sale of the super-Taser. I will tell you now that the prospective buyer of the super-Taser represents a group of anti-government terrorist wannabes calling themselves the 'John Brown Society'. Their stated aim is to cause much disruption of government endeavors, and to make as many people as possible become dissatisfied enough to take up arms in rebellion. They feel that they're called upon by God to correct what they see as injustices.'

'What is this threat against my brother and his family supposed to accomplish?' Jamie blurted out, unable to control herself any longer.

'That is believed to be an order from someone in the leadership of the Golden BBs,' Hugo told her. 'Our inside man believes that there may be, or may have been, a grudge between someone in your families and someone in the past of this leader. The connection is unknown at this time. The supposed aim of this person is to eliminate both of the Holmes and Watson family names from the rosters of future history.'

'But why?' Sam thought he could understand revenge against himself — but a vendetta against Jamie? 'Jamie has no direct link to any of the criminals that I have caused to be incarcerated.'

'Your families, together and separately, have been known for generations to have successfully opposed the criminal minds that had seemed irreproachable,' Hugo answered. 'You, Jamie, and her brother and his family represent the end of the Holmes and Watson families. This person knows that Sherlock Holmes and Doctor John H. Watson were not fictional, and that both have heirs that are alive today. Elimination of those heirs would give their enterprises a psychological boost.'

'Surely,' Jamie countered, 'there were other detective dynasties? Not all of the great mystery detectives of the late nineteenth and early twentieth centuries could have been fictional! Look at the original Holmes and Watson. Their case histories have been read as entertainment for nearly a century and a half. Almost no one believes that either of them sired children, even if they really existed.

'Doctor Watson allowed Sir Arthur Conan Doyle free rein of his imagination, and the use of most of his journals. And yet he and Holmes managed to keep most of their lives private, especially after Holmes retired to his bee-keeping farm in Southern England.'

'True,' Hugo replied. 'Charlie Chan, Phillip Marlowe, and Sam Spade all come to mind. However, they have all proven to be truly fictional. There is no hard evidence that they ever existed outside the imaginations of their creators. No, I'm afraid that of all the great detectives of fictional history, the two of you are the only ones whose ancestors actually existed. They believe that 'Holmes and Watson' have caused all of their setbacks from Moriarty's time until now. They cannot afford to allow you two to become too involved in their affairs now that you have been teamed up.'

'But why did you want to involve me?' R.R. wanted to know. 'I'm just an investigative reporter for a hack newspaper.'

'Like the original Sherlock Holmes and Doctor Watson,' Hugo smiled irritatingly, 'you have a knack for finding out what others wish to keep hidden. As such, you are like a dose of itching powder in their beds. Report your findings as you have always done. The Golden BBs and the John Brown Society will possibly make an open — and fatal for their operations — mistake, and thereby find themselves the victims, rather than the victors.'

Hugo pressed a button on the arm of his wheelchair, and Lydia returned to escort the three of them back to Sam's car. After they were all inside the car, R.R. asked the others, 'What's in this for me? I don't see any profit in this at all. It don't look like a Pulitzer Prize story, either.'

'If you don't end up a test subject,' Jamie said coldly, 'you get to live and write more of your slimy exposés. Maybe you will finally find material for a prizewinning story. I couldn't care less, just as long as James and his family are safe.'

'Take it easy, Jamie,' Sam said soothingly. 'Right now, we need R.R.'s contacts and his newspaper to make these socially inadequate misfits make a mistake that we can exploit. The three of us need to put together an article that will seem as if we know more than we do.

'Jamie, can your brother get your sister-in-law and nephew out of the country quietly until we settle accounts with these individuals?'

'Just this morning,' Jamie was reminded, 'James told me that he had received a research grant to travel to England and study nineteenth-century London. He said that he and his family were planning to sail on the *QE2* early next week.'

'That means that they'll probably take a plane to the East Coast and leave by boat from New York, or one of the other major seaports.' Sam was thinking rapidly. 'Would your brother be opposed to going by plane all the way to Heathrow?'

'I'm not sure how firm his plans are.' Jamie's brow knotted in thought. 'Maybe he would be willing to change his itinerary. I could call him later and let him know what we know. He may have some ideas of his own.'

* * *

Jamie talked with her brother that evening, explaining the dangers of his position. He quickly saw the wisdom of her plans and agreed that a slight change in his travel plans might be an intelligent move.

'Besides,' he told her thoughtfully, 'little Jimmy hasn't been on an ocean cruise before. At his age, he's likely to get fussy about having anything new to do after the first day. The plane trip would only last a matter of hours, and then he'd have doting grandparents and a completely new environment to keep his attention. I think that Alicia would prefer the shorter duration of the plane ride herself. I'll tell her what you just told me, and let you know what we decide. Thanks for your concern, sis.'

Jamie hung up the phone, feeling marginally better about her brother's safety.

I just wish we could find some way to make it look as if James and his family were still going to England by boat, she told herself. *That would help muddy the waters and give him and his family an extra measure of security.*

Knowing that the rest of James' plans were now out of her hands, she began to ponder the need for looking after her own well-being. Of course she had gone through the police academy training, and knew the basics of police procedures and self-defense, but she had had very little practical experience. Perhaps she would ask Sam for pointers. She was beginning to look upon him as a friend as well as a partner and colleague. Perhaps, when this case was over, the department would keep them together.

15

At the station the following morning, Jamie and Sam sat at his desk discussing possible ways of flushing out their enemies.

'How did the phone conversation with your brother go?' Sam inquired. 'Was he willing to change his plans about the ocean cruise?'

'Not only that,' Jamie answered back, 'but he had some very convincing arguments of his own for changing his plans to make to Alicia. If we could somehow make it look as if he and his family were still going to sail to London, I'd feel a lot better. We could use the misdirection to our advantage, I think.'

'I'm inclined to agree with you.' Sam nodded in agreement. 'If James and his family were believed to be on the boat, they might send someone to find an opportunity for mischief of the permanent kind. On board a boat, there would be more time for fortune to work to their advantage. Let's talk to Lieutenant Baker and see what we can set up.'

They walked from Sam's desk across the detectives' room to the lieutenant's office. Once there, they knocked on the open door.

Lieutenant Baker looked up from his phone conversation and waved them in, pointing to the empty chairs in front of his desk. As they sat down, he finished his call and hung up the phone.

'What's on your minds?' His gaze was as questioning as his voice.

They gave him the details of their conversation with Hugo Langsman from the afternoon before, and of Jamie's talks with her brother later.

'We'd like to somehow make it appear that my brother still plans to take the *QE2* to London,' Jamie added. 'Perhaps we could catch someone in the act and turn them in.'

'Now all we need,' Baker told them in a flat tone of voice, 'is a compelling reason, and a budget proposal.'

'I should think that the safety of

civilians,' Sam proposed, 'would be a compelling enough reason. And I have enough money saved to pay for one round-trip ticket.'

'I have enough to pay for the other. And the ticket for a toddler only two years old should be free,' Jamie added.

'That's all well and good,' Lieutenant Baker continued, 'but you two won't be the ones taking the trip. You'll be needed here. Also, these persons will be keeping tabs on you. Jamie will have to be seen traveling to Las Vegas to say goodbye to her brother and his family when their plane leaves for the East Coast. Sam's investigative expertise will be needed to find our suspects and, hopefully, stop this sale.

'We also need the both of you to find out if these Golden BBs have reverse-engineered the super-Taser — or if not, if they have a set of blueprints that they can sell for the mass production of the weapon. We need to prevent this weapon from reaching the street, at least until a defense can be developed.'

The discussion continued for some

time as plans were developed for setting up the decoying away from, and the protection of, Jamie's family.

When everything had been as thoroughly thought out as possible, Jamie called her brother in Las Vegas, and made him aware of their efforts toward the protection of him and his family.

'Alicia was looking forward to the cruise,' he informed her, 'but I think that I've got her convinced of the merits of the shorter travel time by plane. She really didn't want to admit at first that someone could be after our child just because of his ancestors. She's adamant now about putting them away, even if she has to do it herself. Preferably by legal means . . . but she's not averse to using other, more permanent, methods if it's to protect Jimmy.'

'Sam and I are working very hard on the legal means,' was Jamie's reply. 'That's why we want you to fly to London instead of taking the boat.'

Jamie spent the next several minutes relating what she and Sam had discussed with Lieutenant Baker. When she told him how they planned to set up decoys based on their original itinerary, James raised his own question.

They're not planning on using a couple with a real toddler, are they?'

'Not only would that be unconscionably irresponsible of us,' Jamie explained to her brother, 'but it is actually unnecessary, with those lifelike infant and toddler dolls in use to discourage young girls at risk from having sex and getting pregnant while they are way too young. They use sophisticated computer chips programmed to behave realistically like true children. It's supposed to teach girls what a huge responsibility parenthood truly is.'

'As if anyone can actually be prepared!' James replied with a resigned sigh. 'True parenthood is a long-term commitment. I'm glad there's a realistic alternative to using a real child.'

'When are you leaving Las Vegas?' Jamie changed the subject. 'It would be perfectly natural for me to take a few days' leave and come see everyone since you'll be gone so far away and for so long a time.'

'Our plane leaves next Tuesday morning at eight-twenty,' she was told. 'Can you leave tomorrow? That way you'd have four days to spoil Jimmy before we have to leave for London.'

'If I leave around two-thirty in the morning,' Jamie replied cheerfully, 'I'll be there in time to enjoy breakfast with my favorite nephew and his parents. I'll make arrangements with Doctor Cannon and Lieutenant Baker. I'll see if Sergeant Holmes can get some time off to come with me.'

'And I'll have the chance to tell Mom and Dad that I got to meet the descendant of Great-Great-Granddad's partner,' James told her. 'They'd love to hear about him, and about how you and he are a team.'

* * *

Sam and Jamie were approaching the Nevada state line just as the sun was beginning to climb above the horizon.

'Only one or two more hours,' Sam said in conversation, 'and we'll be sitting at your brother's table. I'm looking forward to meeting him and his family.'

'He sounded like he was anxious to meet you, too,' was Jamie's studied reply. 'I don't think any of the Holmes and Watson families have had any real contact since the Korean conflict in the early 1950s.'

'Long enough ago that my father often wondered if all of those stories in the *Strand* weren't mostly fiction,' Sam replied. 'You really surprised me when you said that your great-great-grandfather was *the* Doctor John H. Watson.'

'And no one had ever said that Sherlock Holmes ever married and fathered children. Great-Great-Granddad had always made him seem so indifferent, though polite, to almost all women.'

'That all changed when he met my great-grandmother.'

They soon entered the city's streets of homes and apartments, and Jamie began giving directions to her brother's house.

'Turn left at the next corner,' she advised. 'It'll be the redbrick house with light yellow trim, on the right, about three houses past the corner.'

'This looks like a really nice family neighborhood,' Sam commented as he parked in front of the indicated house. 'Looks like plenty of room for your nephew to play. And maybe have a pet some day.'

'Yes.' Jamie smiled wistfully. 'James and Alicia have talked about getting a medium-sized dog for Jimmy when he's older and more responsible.'

'You sound as if you envy your brother, Jamie.' Sam looked at his partner.

'In a way, I guess I do.' Jamie sighed and shrugged her shoulders. 'James was always the more settled and goal-orientated of the two of us. He always seemed to know what he wanted out of life, and went for it.'

The front door opened. A tall, fit-looking young man of about thirty-five, with dark blond hair and a full, neatly-trimmed mustache, stood in the door frame. As Jamie got out of the car, a broad grin spread across his face and lit a welcoming fire in his hazel-colored eyes.

'You're a little early,' a pleasantly deep

voice greeted them as the young man walked quickly down the walk and gathered Jamie into his firm embrace. 'And this must be Sergeant Holmes.' He held out his hand. His handshake was warm and firm. Sam immediately liked this man.

'Is little Jimmy awake yet?' Jamie inquired of her brother.

'He was almost too excited to last night to go to sleep,' James answered. ''Auntie come! Auntie come!' was all he could say. But I think he'll be up just as soon as he hears your voice. The coffee should be ready by now.'

They walked through the spacious living room and into the large kitchen/dining room. On the Formica countertop a coffee maker was making soft, gurgling sounds as the last of the heated water dripped through the filtered coffee grounds.

'Is unflavored coffee alright, Sam?' James asked, holding the carafe above a large porcelain mug, ready to pour. 'I believe we have some flavored additives if you prefer.'

'Plain is fine,' Sam informed him. 'I actually prefer my coffee just the way you've made it. No creamer, sweetener, or flavoring needed. That's a wonderful color and aroma as well.'

Excited noises were now coming down the hallway.

'Jamie!' The boisterous voice of a young boy and the carpet-muffled heavy foot-steps was heard as he rushed into the dining room. 'You come to see Jimmy, Auntie Jamie. Jimmy happy!'

'How's my big nephew?' Sam watched enviously as Jamie was covered with the happy child's kisses and hugs. 'Would you like to meet my policeman friend, Jimmy? We work together in California.'

Jimmy looked over at Sam.

'Don't see badge. Don't see gun,' Jimmy observed. 'Really policeman?'

'Yes, I am,' Sam told him, sounding serious as he opened his leather wallet and showed his detective badge. 'I left my gun locked in the car. That way, there's no accidents.'

Jimmy seemed satisfied. He got down from Jamie's lap and solemnly stuck out his hand to Sam, saying, 'Pleased to meet you, Mr. Policeman. My name is Jimmy. What's yours?'

'My name is Samuel Holmes, Jimmy.' Sam gravely shook Jimmy's outstretched hand. 'My friends call me 'Sam' when I'm on vacation. Do you want to be my friend?'

'You and Auntie Jamie friends?' Jimmy said when he finished shaking Sam's hand.

'Yes,' Sam told him. 'We work together, just like our ancestors did a long, long time ago.'

'Really? Is true, Auntie Jamie? Is true, Sam?'

'Yes,' Jamie and Sam said together. 'Is really true.'

Just then, a woman with medium-length auburn hair pulled back into a ponytail said from the doorway, 'Little Jimmy, let your Aunt Jamie and her friend finish their coffee, and I'll make you a Mickey Mouse pancake for breakfast.'

'Auntie Jamie's friend named 'Sam',' Jimmy informed her. 'He wants to be my friend, too. Is that okay, Mama?'

'If he'll agree to call me 'Alicia', then you can be his friend and call him 'Sam',' the boy's mother agreed, and then held out her hand towards Sam.

'Pleased to meet you, Alicia.' Sam smiled and shook her proffered hand. 'I was just telling Jimmy about our ancestors having worked together.'

'And so the legend was real.' Alicia eyed her husband and sister-in-law. 'What happens now that Holmes and Watson are once again officially working together?'

'Pretty much what originally happened,' Jamie replied. 'We solve puzzles that others can't, or won't.'

'And that means,' James stroked his chin thoughtfully, 'that there are now unknown enemies after me, Alicia, and Jimmy, as well as yourselves — doesn't it, Jamie?'

'I'm afraid it does, big brother,' Jamie said, her eyes held steadily on his. 'Some people think that the team of Holmes and Watson has been responsible for their failures in the past.'

'But how could they claim that,' Alicia wondered aloud, 'if the families haven't had much contact in two or three generations?'

'I did some research,' James told them, 'after Jamie told me the story of the Golden BBs and their leader's agendas. During the last World War, it seems that a Mycroft Watson was responsible for the break-up of an intelligence brokerage ring in and around greater London. Then, during the Korean War, a young police officer in the United States, named Jason Holmes, captured several black-marketeers operating within the military and civil services.

'And Dad, before he became one of the leading medical teachers at UCLA, helped an unnamed undercover agent to track down an early group of bioterrorists and destroy their operation. Dad never talked about that period of his life, and I had no idea that he had ever been involved in counterespionage of any kind.

'It would seem that the descendants of Sherlock Holmes and Doctor John H. Watson have carved out their own niche in the history of crime-fighting. And now, a new batch of masterminds has lain out their own plans to get rid of their traditional nemeses. I think it would be wise to alert Dad and Mom just as soon as we arrive in the UK.'

'There seems to be a lot that we have never known about our own families,' Sam summarized for everyone. 'How much detail do you think we can dig up in the few days we have before you leave for London, James?'

'I don't know,' was James's response. 'A lot of information is still classified. We would need clearances from several different government and law enforcement agencies before we could do any major deep searches.'

'We have some special clearances from the FBI and the military. Do you think Colonel Rembrandt and SAC Jones could get us the clearance levels to access those records?' Jamie asked.

'With what we've already found out, I think it is within the realm of possibility,' was Sam's studied reply. 'It's worth a try. We really need that data. Especially if we are to defend ourselves and our families.'

'I'll see how deep James and I can get

into what's available on the internet,' Jamie added. 'The more we find out on our own, the less we'll have to dig out from the bureaucracies, and the quicker we will have the information we need.'

After breakfast, everyone went about their assignments.

'I wanna help,' Jimmy kept saying. 'Bad guys need to be put inna corner and made to feel bad about hurting people!'

'They need more than that, Jimmy,' his mother told him. 'They need to be put away where they can't hurt people anymore.'

16

Sam used his cellphone to contact Lieutenant Baker while Jamie visited with her brother and played board games with her nephew. When Lieutenant Baker called back a short time later, Sam had taken his new friend Jimmy to the nearby park, and was watching him use the combination climbing-frame-and-slide designed to look like an old-time fort. Sam reached for his cellphone when he felt it vibrating in his pocket. He checked the caller ID and then flipped it open to receive the call.

'Sergeant Holmes,' he answered as Jimmy rushed up to him all excited.

'Sam!' The boy was out of breath from climbing up the rope ladder, sliding down the slide, and running. 'Did you see me climb that rope ladder like the big kids and come down the slide? I got alla way to the top!'

'Yes I did, Jimmy.' Sam smiled at the

exuberant and excited little boy. 'You're a great little climber!'

'Is this a bad time, Sergeant Holmes?' the voice on the phone chuckled.

'No, Lieutenant,' Sam answered. 'I'm at the playground with Jamie's nephew while she and her brother and his wife make plans to elude discovery of the change in their itinerary when they reach New York. How are things going at your end?'

'Special Agent in Charge Jones has two agents ready to leave Nevada for the New York harbor on a flight shortly after the Watsons' take-off. They'll board the *QE2* using the Watsons' boarding passes and wearing identical clothing. A toddler-simulation doll will be in a stroller. While they travel, the doll will either be in its stroller or in the cabin, allegedly asleep or playing games. A cover story of mild seasickness will be used to keep others from wondering why the child's not more active.

'Professor Watson, his wife, Doctor Watson, and you will receive an invitation to a *Bon Voyage* supper at the home of a colleague. The agents will be at the house.

While you're there, all of you can make final plans for the trip.'

'That sounds like as good a plan as any,' Sam said and then asked, 'Have Jamie and I received the upgraded security clearances we were hoping for?'

Lieutenant Baker laid the receiver down as he checked the papers that had just been placed upon his desk. After quickly scanning them, he picked it up again.

'It just came through,' he told Sam. 'You, Jamie, her parents, brother, and sister-in-law have been given top-level clearances. There's even one for Doctor Watson's father from British intelligence. Apparently, the British have also been looking into the activities of the Golden BBs, and found that the elder Watson's father did some undercover work for them during the war.'

Sam and his boss disconnected. 'Time to go home now, kiddo,' Sam told Jimmy and took the boy's hand as they walked back to the house.

★　★　★

On Sunday Prof. Watson received an invitation from the Dean of English history to a farewell dinner at his residence the following evening. Coffee would be served at 5:30 with dinner at 6:00. James said that he and his family would be there and asked if it would be alright to bring his sister and her friend who were visiting with him just before he left for his long stay in the English countryside. After having been told to bring whomever he wished, he was asked how many people to expect for dinner.

'There will be five of us with little Jimmy,' James responded. 'It's pretty short notice to get a sitter.'

'How old is your son now?' the dean asked. 'He's getting to be a big boy isn't he?'

'Yes, he is,' James told him. 'His third birthday is next weekend. My parents will have the chance to celebrate it with him this year.'

'Then he and my grandson should get along just fine.' The dean's voice sounded pleased. 'Kevin just turned four. He and my daughter and son-in-law from New

York have been visiting this week.'

'That sounds great,' James agreed. 'We'll look forward to seeing you tomorrow evening.'

When James disconnected, he told Sam and Jamie about his conversation.

'Dean Samuelson never married,' he told them, 'so he doesn't have a daughter, or a grandson that I've ever heard of. They must be the agents that your lieutenant told you to expect.'

'Yes,' Sam said, 'that would be a logical conclusion. That would help explain their presence in case anyone is watching us.'

'And what better way to introduce a small child than to say that he belonged to someone you would have reason to have contact with and who would be leaving for the East Coast at about the same time,' Jamie added.

Alicia came in to call everyone to dinner. James told her about the next night's dinner invitation.

Jimmy was excited about getting to be out late with the grown-ups, but was a little confused about the toddler-simulation doll. He asked lots of questions about how the 'baby' could be like him, but not be real. He couldn't understand why two grown-ups wanted to play with children's toys.

'It's used to make people think that a child is with them when it would be dangerous to use a real child, Jimmy,' Sam was trying to explain. 'Sometimes bad people want to hurt the parents and don't care if the child gets hurt too. This way, the police can catch the bad people and the child doesn't get hurt. The real parents are out of danger, too, because police officers are pretending to be the people that the bad people want to hurt.'

'So, bad guys can't hurt little kid?' Jimmy wanted to know.

'No,' James told his son. 'Only the police officers could get hurt. But they're trained to be careful and act smart.'

'Besides,' Jamie told him, 'it's their jobs to be in the dangerous places to protect all of the little Jimmies and their parents.'

'And their Auntie Jamies, too?' Jimmy wanted to know.

'And their Auntie Jamies, too,' Sam told him.

17

The next evening, Jimmy got to see how the simulation toddler was used. He was fascinated by its behavior. He knew that the doll couldn't talk to him, but he enjoyed pretending that it reacted to his questions. The dinner was enjoyable and the conversation was kept light. After Jimmy fell asleep on the couch, the adults began to discuss plans for the next day.

'The Watsons' plane is scheduled for 8:20 in the morning,' Agent Thorsdatter, the female FBI agent, told them. 'Agent Roberts and I will be leaving on the Eastern Airlines flight at 9:00. We should each arrive in New York about three hours later in New York. Agent Roberts and I will check into the hotel and wait for our boarding time the next day. The Watson party, using the name Josephson, will wait for their connecting flight to Heathrow Airport in London.

'If all goes as planned, Prof. Watson and his family will land in London at its scheduled time, to be picked up by a limo company displaying their assumed name. From there they will be taken to a local hotel and the parents will meet them in the hotel's restaurant later. The next day, the elder Watsons will drive them to their home. Hopefully, at the good doctor's home, they will be safe until this has all blown over.'

'I'll just be glad when we can all breathe easier,' Alicia said with feeling.

'Working on that as quickly as possible,' Agent Roberts agreed.

*   *   *

The next morning, James, Alicia, and Jimmy, all of whom had stayed overnight at Dean Samuelson's home while the agents had accompanied Sam and Jamie to Prof. Watson's home, were taken to the airport in the dean's car. They arrived with plenty of time to check their luggage and pick up the tickets waiting for them at the counter.

With everything done and their boarding passes in hand, they waited in the lounge for their flight to be called for the boarding of passengers with Dean Samuelson.

'It's a shame you have to miss being with your family during the last half-hour before you leave the country,' Samuelson commented. 'It's not the same as going overseas for a vacation. You'll be gone for six months to a year. That's a long time for someone as young as Jimmy.'

'Long enough for him to sound like a true Brit,' Alicia laughed.

'Will he still remember your sister, James?' the dean asked.

'He's too attached to her, I think,' James replied, 'to forget her at this point. When she visits for a long weekend, they are almost inseparable. I think that, given the way he took to Sam, it wouldn't take very long for them to bond as well.'

'Yes,' agreed Alicia. 'He and Jamie seem to be well matched, don't you think? They'll make great partners, too.'

★ ★ ★

Later, Sam, Jamie, and the FBI agents with their toddler-sim, rode to the airport in Jamie's car.

'Do you think James and his family will arrive safely at Heathrow?' Sam inquired with apparent calm in his voice. 'Is there anything we have left undone or haven't thought of?'

'Second-guessing the plans, Sergeant?' Agent Thorsdatter raised an eyebrow as she looked at him.

'No,' Sam told her. 'Just thinking of a couple of old saws. You know, the ones about 'the best laid plans of mice and men' and 'no battle plan survives contact with the enemy'. We've kept everything as simple as we could, but there are still a lot of variables.'

'Well,' Jamie added as she drove, 'there's always divine intervention.'

They arrived at the airport loading zone and got help from a Skycap with the luggage.

'Eastern Airlines flight for JFK,' they told him. Jamie went to park he car as the others followed the Skycap to the counter.

As they sat down to wait for their flight to be called, Sam kept an eye on the crowd in the snack bar. Agent Roberts waved to Jamie as she entered the waiting area. She joined them and everyone appeared to be making small talk.

'Security had to escort a loud, aggressive woman spouting some sort of doomsday doctrine for all of the sinners who were invading the domain of the birds and flying insects,' Jamie reported as she sat down. 'I haven't heard anything about that before. Have any of you?'

'That sounds like something you might hear in one of Southern California's airports,' Thorsdatter replied. 'Isn't that where all of those kooky cults come from?'

'It does seem so,' Sam added, 'doesn't it? Unfortunately, craziness is not limited to just one geographical location.'

They chatted amicably until the flight to New York was called. Then Jamie gave hugs and kisses to her 'family', and Sam shook hands all around.

'Have a safe trip,' Jamie told them. 'Give my love to Mom and Dad.'

'We will,' Agent Roberts said as he kissed her on the cheek just as James would have done. 'And don't forget to write or call once in a while. You do have international calling on your cellphone, don't you?'

'I've been using it ever since Mom and Dad moved to England,' she agreed. 'I call them at least once a week.'

'So do we,' Agent Thorsdatter lied. 'Jimmy will be thrilled to hear your voice, I'm sure of it.'

Jamie and Sam watched the two FBI agents board the plane and then walked out to the parking lot to get to Jamie's car.

'I wish we could have been here when James and his family left and really said 'goodbye' to them.' Jamie was already missing her brother and his family. 'Jimmy is going to be so much bigger when they return.'

'I really liked them,' Sam said sadly. 'I wish that I'd had more time to get to know them.'

The drive back to California was uneventful until they stopped about halfway back to London at the Hart's Café for a break from driving and to stretch their legs while they filled the fuel tank.

As Sam pumped his gas, he noticed a luxury SUV at the pump aisle next to him. The vehicle had Nevada license plates, and he was positive that it had been following them since they had left the airport.

Sam memorized the number, intending to check it out with the Nevada DMV at his first opportunity for any information that he could find.

Sam paid for the fuel and parked the car at the café where Jamie was sitting, sipping iced tea at a booth. He joined her and also ordered an iced tea.

'Have you noticed that SUV over at the gas station?' he asked Jamie. 'I think that it may have been following us since we left the airport.'

'Or they may just be taking the same route to California,' she observed. 'There aren't that many highways leading from Las Vegas to Riverside County or Los Angeles after all.'

'I'm sure I saw it behind us as we pulled out of the parking lot,' was his comment. 'Better to be prepared than to be surprised.'

'I'll keep an eye out for him while you drive the rest of the way home,' was all she had to say.

The SUV that they had been talking about pulled into the café's parking lot and parked in a space near their car. As the driver got out, he seemed to take a casual interest in their vehicle as he walked by it as he approached the entrance.

'Does he look familiar?' Sam asked as the man walked toward the restrooms.

'Not to me,' Jamie replied. 'Where do you think that you saw him?'

'Just fleeting glimpses,' Sam closed his eyes in concentration, 'as he twice drove by me firing his weapon. Those acne scars and hatchet face are very memorable.'

'I must have missed him each time,' she told Sam. 'You're certain that's him?'

'As certain as I can be under the circumstances.'

'I'll call Lieutenant Baker as soon as

we're back on the road.'

Sam and Jamie finished their iced teas just as the man from the SUV came from the back and headed to the lunch counter. They got up and paid their tab at the cash register and got into Jamie's car to leave. As they were getting back onto the freeway, Jamie saw the SUV leave the parking lot.

'That was a fast stop,' Jamie commented. 'Either he just needed to use the facilities, or he took his order to go, or doesn't want to lose us. Can you ditch him?'

'If we can reach the next off-ramp before he spots us,' Sam began planning his next move, 'maybe I can come up behind him before he realizes that we're now following him instead of him following us.'

'It's worth a try,' Jamie agreed. 'At least he'll know that he's been made and maybe back off. He'll probably try to pick us up somewhere else after he believes that we think we lost him.'

Sam reached the next exit before their tail caught up with them, and left the freeway to find a place to watch for him. As they waited, they soon saw their quarry go by just slightly above the speed of the traffic flow. Sam quickly got back onto the freeway as Jamie kept an eye on their target. Sam stayed back a few car lengths, and remained in a different lane as they followed the vehicle with the Nevada license plates. After a few miles, the SUV left the freeway and apparently headed back to Las Vegas.

'He has either given up, or plans to find us later at our homes,' Jamie surmised. 'Either way, our enemies know where to find us.'

'That's true,' Sam had to agree. 'I wish there was some way we could go pre-emptive and nail these guys and gals once and for all.'

They didn't see any sign of the luxury SUV during the rest of the trip home, even though Sam and Jamie both kept looking.

Sam pulled Jamie's car into her designated parking space and walked her up to her door.

'You can use the phone inside to call a

cab,' she told him, 'and then wait in an air-conditioned room until it arrives.'

Sam thanked her as she unlocked her door. When she pushed the door open, she stepped back with a squeak of surprise. Sam looked over her shoulder, pulled the door closed, and took out his cellphone and dialed the emergency number.

'911,' the voice answered. 'What is your emergency?'

'This is Sergeant Holmes, London Police Department. I wish to report a B and E with vandalism at the apartment of Doctor Jamesina Watson. The address is 916 Sutton Drive, Apartment A. I am requesting a full investigative team. The burglary may be related to an ongoing case.'

'Please remain at the scene and stay on the line. Units are being called and will be on their way directly.'

Sam and Jamie sat down on a nearby bench. Jamie shed tears of frustration and anger at the violation of her home.

'I want these SOBs in jail and under the highest security!' she almost screamed. 'First they try to kill my partner before I even get to know him, then they threaten my family, and now they invade my home and destroy my sense of safety! I want these people, Sam! I want them like I never wanted anything, or anyone, before!'

Sam put his arm around her shoulder and let her head rest on his chest as he made comforting noises until the police and forensic units arrived. Lieutenant Baker and Doctor Cannon arrived just as two plainclothes officers stepped out of their car. The uniformed officers had already begun to secure the scene and the forensics team was unloading their equipment from their van.

'Sergeant Holmes?' the taller of the two detectives inquired. 'Can you or Doctor Watson supply us with any information about the break-in? You implied that it may be related to a case that you are working on?'

'That's right, Detective . . . ' Sam replied.

'Detective Johns,' the tall detective said. 'And this is my partner, Detective Smyth.'

Sam told them how they had begun to

investigate three seemingly unrelated deaths, how an overheard conversation of a reporter from a tabloid paper had been related to their findings, and how that had led them to a group of gun-running terrorists. Then Jamie told them about the FBI and military connection and that they had learned of a plot against Sam, Jamie, and her family.

Jamie also told them about their long weekend with her brother before he left for his assignment in the UK and how they attempted to throw their pursuers off their trail.

Then they both related the incident of the SUV following them from the airport in Las Vegas until they were able to turn the tables on their follower and began to follow him.

'You say that you saw him at the café,' Johns asked for clarity's sake, 'and that you recognized him as someone who had made at least two attempts on your life. Can you describe him for us?'

'His face was thin with a lot of acne scars,' Sam recalled the man's features. 'And he was about six feet tall and weighed about two hundred pounds. He held his left shoulder as if it had been injured recently. His complexion looked as if he sunburned easily. His hair was the color of baked clay. I didn't get a look at his eyes because he was wearing dark glasses when he was at the gas station and when he walked into the café.'

'It sounds like you got a good enough look to give our sketch artist something to work with,' Smyth commented.

'I'd be willing to give it a go,' was Sam's reply.

After the investigators dusted the apartment for prints and checked for any DNA traces, Jamie was asked to ascertain if anything was missing. She looked quickly at her things.

'Well,' she told the detectives, 'I can tell that one of my flash drives and an information DVD are missing for sure, but a lot of things have been badly smashed. I would have to have more time to say what else might be gone and what was in those missing files. We happened to take my laptop with us because I had just added a couple of new games I thought my nephew might like to have before he left for England. That's still out in the trunk of my car.'

'How long were you in the airport?' Smyth wanted to know.

'It was, what, maybe forty-five minutes from the time we parked until we left the airport area?' Jamie looked at Sam for conformation.

'Something like that,' he assured her.

'And have you checked the luggage area since you left your brother's house?' Jones questioned. 'That's plenty of time for a professional thief to break into the trunk without leaving noticeable evidence at the scene, especially if you were not expecting anything.'

'But maybe we should have.' Sam was angry with himself for not thinking of that first.

'Look at it this way,' Smyth said, correctly interpreting the look on Sam's face and in the tone of his voice. 'If the perpetrators decided to leave you a present and you'd opened it at the airport, we might not be having this conversation.'

Smyth called the bomb squad as Johns called one of the forensics team over to the car before they left. She checked for any new scratches around the lock and the trunk's latch before asking if the vehicle had a trunk release on the inside.

'As a matter of fact, it does, Detective,' she answered.

Sharon, the forensics expert, checked the window areas on each of the front doors for signs that a jimmy had been used. Neither door showed any sign of a break-in. There were no discernable prints on the trunk release.

'I really didn't expect to find anything,' Sharon explained. 'These are all areas that get a lot of use, and a car thief's tools don't leave many traces. If you're thinking that someone could have planted a bomb in the trunk, I'd let the bomb squad open it.'

When the bomb squad arrived, they first allowed the bomb sniffing canine check the inside of the car thoroughly, and then carefully check the outside of the trunk. Again the canine was allowed to sniff the entire car. The dog gave every indication that the vehicle was bomb-free.

After the back area of Jamie's car was covered with a heavy Kevlar quilt as a safety precaution, one of the bomb squad used Jamie's key to unlock the trunk. The trunk was checked for trip wires or any other signs that the area had been tampered with. When the 'all clear' had been given, the trunk was fully opened.

'Okay, Doctor Watson,' the officer told her, 'go ahead and see if anything has been disturbed or is missing.'

Jamie carefully opened her suitcases and her laptop carrier, and Sam did the same with his suitcases.

Finding everything apparently to have been undisturbed, Jamie booted up her computer. Nothing happened. The screen had lit up, but it only showed a blue-colored background. None of her pre-programmed or programmed files were available.

'I think someone scrambled my hard drive!' she exclaimed and began to curse, which was the best evidence of how distraught she was. 'Everything we had theorized and had been able to gather hard evidence on was saved to that hard drive.'

'Didn't you back up those files?' the officer asked.

'The DVD and flash drive that are missing *were* my back-ups,' she said in frustration. 'At least my hidden external hard drive seems not to have been have been touched.'

'How fortunate, then,' Sam grinned, taking out a mini-DVD from a pouch attached to his belt, 'that you let me make a back-up of the back-up. An accountant friend of mine said that he always made at least two extra back-ups to his clients' files and put them in separate places until the files were no longer needed by the IRS or anyone else. It seemed a good idea at the time, so I asked you for my own copy to work on when something came to mind that I wanted to check on. Remember?'

'Samuel Holmes — ' Jamie glared at him, and then broke into a smile. ' — you are a devious scoundrel. But a loveable one, so you're forgiven.'

'That's all well and good,' Lieutenant

Baker interjected, 'but after what happened here, I think that we should check Sergeant Holmes's house as soon as possible.'

Lieutenant Baker used his cellphone to have another forensics team and bomb crew meet him at the young detective's home. They then took the lieutenant's car to Sam's house.

'I want a thorough and complete check of your place, especially your desktop and removable data storage,' Lieutenant Baker told Sam. 'We need to know exactly what is missing or has been tampered with. These people have proven themselves to be ruthless and without mercy many times over.'

The bomb squad had already arrived and checked the door and windows to Sam's place, declaring it safe for forensics to check for signs of forced or other forms of illegal entry. When no scratches were found on the door locks or gouges in the door or window frames, Sam was allowed to cautiously unlock and open his door.

After Jamie's apartment, Sam was expecting more of the same at his home.

His place had definitely been well searched, but not with the wanton destruction that Jamie's had suffered. Did the perpetrators believe that Jamie would be more easily intimidated?

Before Sam switched on his computer, he looked at the back of the CPU tower. The connecting cables were gone! His landline phone had also been unplugged and the cord had been cut into several pieces.

'Check the connectors and the phone,' he suggested to the forensics team leader. 'This is where they may have been the least careful about leaving evidence. They had no need to hurry if they knew how long Doctor Watson and I would be gone, so we may not find anything.'

'One can always hope, Sergeant,' the team leader replied. 'It's human nature to slip up somewhere.'

⋆　⋆　⋆

After both abodes had been thoroughly gone over, and Jamie and Sam had inventoried all of their possessions, they, the team leaders of both forensics teams and both bomb squads, Doctor Cannon, and Lieutenant Backer assembled in the squad meeting room.

'I won't know until I replace the power cords and USB connector cables what may have been done to my computer,' Sam informed the group. 'Once Doctor Watson has used her external hard drive to reset the one in her laptop, she will be able to check for other sabotage to her laptop. My place was not vandalized the way hers was, but I did find that some mementos and some semi-valuable articles missing. The mementos were valuable only to me and the other items are easily replaced.'

Jamie spoke next.

'With the exception of the flash drive and the infodisk, nothing was removed from my apartment. Everything was either smashed or ruined in some way. I agree with Sergeant Holmes that the actions taken in my apartment were intended to intimidate me the same way that the implied threats to members of my family were. No permanent damage appears to have been done to my computer. If Sergeant Holmes had not made an extra copy of our notes on this case, we may have been made to repeat most of our investigation. As it is, we are merely temporarily inconvenienced.'

'The first thing,' one of the forensics team leaders suggested, 'when the computers are working again, is to check thoroughly for any signs of worms, viruses, Trojan horses, logic bombs, et cetera, left in the systems or implanted on any of the doctor's or sergeant's removable storage devices.'

Everyone agreed that should be the next logical step. The meeting was adjourned and each person went back to their jobs.

18

Aboard the *QE2*, Agent Roberts showed Agent Thorsdatter the cablegram that he had received just as they were boarding.

'*Special packages arrived London. No damages or encumbrances,*' it read.

'This implies that the first part of our plan has succeeded,' Thorsdatter commented. 'Let's hope that the rest succeeds as well.'

Just then, the toddler-sim indicated that it was hungry.

'Okay, Jimmy,' Agent Roberts told it. 'We'll check out the snack bar. How would you like a grilled cheese sandwich?'

'How will we simulate 'Jimmy' eating the sandwich?' wondered Thorsdatter.

'We can cut it into finger-food size pieces and eat them ourselves while the sim appears to consume them itself,' Roberts explained. 'It's programmed to look like it is chewing. When it needs to 'go potty', one of us takes it to one of the restrooms and cleans as necessary.'

'This is too weird for me.' Thorsdatter shook her head. 'These machines are getting too sophisticated for me.'

'Even so,' Roberts observed, 'they are still just dolls, and someone could easily identify it as a construct. I think that maybe tomorrow Jimmy should start feeling the effects of motion sickness. Maybe even have a touch of a twenty-four-hour virus.'

'That will cover us for a few days,' Thorsdatter agreed. 'But how will we handle the rest of the voyage?'

'We'll think of something,' Roberts told her. 'Meanwhile, I'll have a word with the ship's doctor and the captain. We will need their help soon anyway.'

★   ★   ★

James, Alicia, and Jimmy arrived at Heathrow Airport on time. A British undercover officer was waiting for them holding a sign that read 'Josephson'.

'That must be our ride to the hotel.' Alicia was the first to see the sign. 'Would you like to ride in a limousine, Jimmy?'

'What's that?' he wondered.

'It's a special car,' she told him, 'just like the governor rides in.'

'We spec'l, Mama?'

'Yes, Jimmy, we are. Very 'spec'l'.'

As they approached the driver, James introduced himself and his family as the Josephson party, and they shook hands.

'Very good, sir,' the man replied. 'If you will give me your baggage claim, I'll see that it is put in the boot.'

'Where boot, Mama?' Jimmy was fascinated. 'No see a boot.'

'That's what they call the trunk over here,' his father informed him. 'They also call the hood a 'bonnet'.'

'Cars don't wear clothes.' Jimmy giggled. 'That's silly!'

'Maybe to you and me, son,' James told him, 'but that's the way they do things here in England.'

'What do they call the engine?'

'The engine.'

The driver came back, and the luggage was brought over to the limousine on a cart. After it was loaded, the 'Josephsons' got into the backseat and the driver got behind the wheel.

Jimmy looked at the driver with a disturbed visage. When asked by his mother what was wrong, Jimmy whispered to her that the man was driving from the wrong side of the car. Alicia explained to him that it was because English people drove on the other side of the road from people in the US.

'English people are funny,' Jimmy commented with a laugh.

The limousine pulled into the unloading area of the hotel. A liveried doorman greeted them and called for a porter to unload the luggage onto a cart.

James approached the desk and made inquiries about their rooms.

'We have reservations for one night for two adults and a child,' he told the desk clerk, 'under the name of Josephson. We'll be staying with relatives after tonight.'

'Your rooms are ready,' he was told by the desk clerk. 'And your relatives have already arrived. They are waiting in the hotel's restaurant and bar. I'll have your suitcases sent to your rooms, and have you shown to your table and let your party know that you have arrived.'

James thanked the desk clerk and tipped the bellhop. The maître d' was quickly by their sides, and led them to a table where a couple was already being seated. Smiles broke out on everyone's faces as they were seated.

'So,' the elder Watson said as he embraced his son and daughter-in-law, 'this is the grandson I haven't seen since his first birthday! Will you give your Grandpa and Grandma a hug, Jimmy?'

'You my Grandpa and Grandma?' Jimmy inquired with a curious look on his face. 'Mama and Papa said that we would be visiting. You really Papa's mommy and daddy?'

'And your Aunt Jamie's too.' Mrs. Watson beamed at him as she gave him a hug. 'I hear that your third birthday will be soon. Would you like a party at our house?'

As they ate, the Watsons all caught up on the current family gossip. James explained how Jamie and Sam had been partnered together, and how they had been made aware of the vendetta against both families.

'Sam says that he is the last with the Holmes' name,' Alicia explained, 'however, his parents both had cousins on their mothers' sides of the family. And of course you're aware of your own family history.'

'Yes, there has always been a strong 'Moriarty Syndrome',' Doctor Watson observed. 'The Holmes and Watson names have always drawn the attention of master criminals and their wannabes, much to their undoing.'

Jimmy yawned sleepily and it was decided to continue the conversation later the next day after they were at the home of Doctor and Mrs. Watson. Since the elder Watsons were staying at a local bed and breakfast overnight, it was agreed that they would meet the younger Watsons and drive them to their home in the country after breakfast.

'We live on the property where Sherlock Holmes raised his bees after he retired from consulting,' Doctor Watson informed the younger members of his family. 'There's even a neighbor whose family has tended the hives for generations after the old detective and his young wife left for the States before the Blitz.'

*   *   *

Life aboard the *QE2* seemed normal enough. The weather itself seemed to cooperate in making it a pleasant voyage. Agent Roberts and Agent Thorsdatter had taken turns giving credence to the story that their son was ill and fussy. The ship's doctor and the captain, once they were told about the FBI agents' mission, were quite helpful.

The ship's doctor visited his young 'patient' every day late in the morning and brought games and toys to keep the toddler occupied since he wasn't allowed to leave the cabin. The other passengers were told that the boy had a cold that was aggravated by motion sickness and was running a mild fever. He was expected to recover by the time the ship made port in Great Britain.

While the ship was still a day or two

out from port, Roberts had become aware that one of the stewards seemed to always be around in the passageways, with seemingly little to do. When he asked the doctor who the steward was, the doctor didn't know, and said that the man must be new this trip. The captain couldn't offer any news except that he did not seem to be on the ship's roster.

'He may be someone sent to spy on us,' Agent Thorsdatter posited. 'We may have succeeded in our little ruse.'

'I think we'd better keep an eye on this particular steward,' was Agent Roberts' studied reply.

★ ★ ★

At two o'clock the next morning, ship's time, Roberts and Thorsdatter were awakened by a bright light coming from the sitting area of their cabin. An acrid odor and a sharp crackle of sound were also observed through the hallway to the sofa and the reading chair. Roberts grabbed the fire extinguisher and pushed the fire emergency button on the intra-ship phone. Thorsdatter grabbed the toddler-sim, wrapped it in some blankets, and followed behind Roberts as he cleared a safe path to the door through the smoky flames.

When they reached the outside, they both began yelling 'fire' and pounding on their neighbors' doors.

The ship's emergency crew arrived very quickly and was given directions to the fire.

'We need to take our child to the infirmary,' Roberts said in the worried voice of a concerned and panicky parent. 'He's been having a bad time during the trip, and the smoke couldn't have helped him any.'

The first mate called the infirmary and made certain that the doctor and the captain would meet them there.

'As soon as the fire is cold,' the first mate explained, 'we'll start our investigation into how the fire started and find out why there was no alarm set off. This is completely unheard of, Professor Watson, I assure you.'

'And the repercussions could be

far-reaching, I'm sure,' Roberts, in his role of Professor James Watson, said coldly. 'Especially if negligence is involved.'

As soon as everyone arrived at the infirmary, 'little Jimmy' was taken to a private room and given a 'thorough examination' by the doctor under the watchful eyes of his parents and the captain.

'It's almost certain,' the captain was saying, 'that the fire was deliberately set.'

'Has anyone recognized the steward that we saw lurking around our cabin?' Roberts inquired impatiently. 'There's nowhere to go on the ship.'

'But there are plenty of places to hide,' the doctor added. 'The *QE2* is a very large ship with lots of places where a person could get lost in the crowd. Passengers and crew add up to the population of a small city.'

'And that gives our suspect plenty of ways to conceal his identity,' the captain reluctantly admitted. 'There's no way to find this person in the time left before landfall.'

'Can we say that our 'child' is in a

guarded, but stable, condition?' Thorsdatter wanted to know. 'Some kind of notice that might draw out the perpetrator — or perpetrators — before we reach port?'

'I think that we might be able to arrange that,' the captain agreed.

It was decided that 'little Jimmy' would stay under medical surveillance until the ship landed. Then his 'parents' would take him to the local hospital for a final examination and evaluation. Everyone involved thought this would provide their attacker with an opportunity to strike at the member of the Watson family least able to defend himself and to do the most emotional damage to the others.

Since this was planned as a trap to catch a member of the Golden BBs gang or the John Brown Society in the act of attempted assassination, Roberts and Thorsdatter believed that they would apprehend their quarry before reaching British soil.

The infirmary room was watched twenty-four hours a day by Agent Roberts, Agent Thorsdatter, or the first mate. The ship's doctor and the captain were the only other individuals allowed unhindered access into the 'child's' sick room.

The last evening before disembarking was one of gaiety and partying. The passengers were also celebrating the fact that the fire had been limited just to the Watsons' cabin and that no one had been seriously injured. The reports on the youngest Watson were positive, and both parents were able to join the festivities for an hour or two while the child slept under the watchful eyes of the first mate and the doctor.

It was approaching midnight when the first mate and the doctor thought that they heard the muffled sound of glass breaking. Thinking that the intruder might use some kind of a gas bomb to disable the child's protectors, the doctor and the first mate had donned surgical masks treated with a solution that would provide a limited immunity to such an attack

After a few minutes to allow the air to clear, the door was quietly opened. A short man with dark hair and a wrestler's build — and, in the dark, matching Roberts' description of the strange steward — slipped into the infirmary. Using an infrared lantern and wearing special goggles, he worked his way into the sickroom.

The masks had given a little protection from the gas, but even so, the doctor and first mate were feeling a little woozy. The man aimed a weapon at the bed and fired just as the two protectors grabbed his arm and spoiled his shot. There was a sizzle to the air as if an electrical charge had been fired, and a quiet thump on the pillow of the bed. The child (in actuality, the toddler-sim) started crying and making a huge fuss. Because of the effects of the gas intended to disable the child's guardians, the attacker was able to elude his would-be captors, slip out into the night, and get away.

Having made sure that nothing was wrong with the toddler-sim, the first mate contacted the captain, who found the 'Watsons' and rushed to the infirmary.

'He got away,' the doctor informed them when they arrived. He and the first mate were out in the fresh air recovering from their bout with the knock-out gas.

'Our reflexes were slowed down by the gas that made it past the antidote solution,' the first mate added with a faint wheeze. 'I'm uncertain if he picked up on your ruse with the simulacrum. He was very busy trying to escape.'

'Were you able to get a good look at the perpetrator?' Thorsdatter questioned anxiously. 'Was there anything that would identify him? If he gets off of the ship, he can get lost in the city until he's ready to strike again.'

'And if,' the captain was quick to point out, 'he saw through the deception, he could also tell his co-conspirators back in the US. The real Watsons could be in danger.'

'We'll notify our opposite numbers here in the UK.' Roberts looked grave. 'The older Watson has had experience in the world of intrigue. He'll be the most likely member of the family to become aware of any problems once he's been made aware of the situation.'

The captain recommended that a

radiogram be sent immediately to Scotland Yard and the Ministry of Intelligence, acquainting them with the situation as it now stood. The FBI agents agreed, and were prepared to continue their decoy mission.

'We also need to notify the Bureau and the detectives involved in the case,' Thorsdatter advised. 'Doctor Jamesina Watson has a personal involvement in the situation.'

The messages were hastily sent and everyone went to bed so as to be awake and alert early for the next day's departure after the ship passed its customs inspections. The tension was evident in the two agents' demeanors. Neither of them was able to rest easy during the rest of the night.

They were awakened two hours after dawn by the ship's PA system alerting the passengers to have their luggage packed and ready for inspection and removal to the docks.

'A good thing that little Jimmy was able to 'sleep well',' Roberts said, with his hand covering a jaw-cracking yawn. 'He'll be ready to greet all of the new experiences of the London on this side of the Atlantic.'

'After all of the excitement of last night,' Thorsdatter agreed, hiding a yawn of her own as she finished packing her last suitcase, 'I'm surprised that he slept at all. All I know is that I could only sleep in little naps all night.'

'At least coming by ship, we won't have to deal with jet lag.'

'Only the after-effects of a poor night's sleep.'

19

When Sam and Jamie were given the news from the *QE2*, they were concerned, but not too surprised. The FBI agents were still playing their part in hopes of gaining another chance to catch the elusive assassin.

Jamie's laptop had checked out free of any devastating problems. Sam's desktop was re-hooked to its power source by a new cord, and the connector cables were easily replaced. When he booted up his computer, the system came back up without any problems, and checked out free of any disabling files or programs.

The back-up mini-DVD that he had made also showed no signs of tampering.

'That was to be expected,' Jamie said as they discussed the news in Lieutenant Baker's office, 'since the mini-disk had never left the sergeant's person except to be viewed. And even then, it was never out of his sight.'

'Now, what can we do here,' was Doctor Cannon's question, 'to help the situation over there?'

'We keep searching for the headquarters of the Golden BBs and the John Brown Society.' Lieutenant Baker frowned as he made his comment.

'Didn't John Brown's career end at the Harper's Ferry Federal Arsenal?' Sam asked. 'Perhaps they're planning some sort of action there in relation to a historical event.'

'In which case,' Jamie answered, 'we ought to check the historical records and the encyclopedia for information.'

'Simple enough,' Lieutenant Baker told them. 'I'll have the research department check on it while you two check on the man that followed you from the Las Vegas Airport. Your description matches both of the twin brothers who call themselves 'Cain' and 'Seth'. The man who died in the parking garage shoot-out was another brother who has been identified as 'Abel'.'

'The three sons of Adam and Eve mentioned in Genesis?' Jamie's interest perked up. 'And it was Abel that Cain killed in the earliest known murder. Very interesting, even if it is only a coincidence.'

Jamie and Sam were informed that the three brothers were known associates of a 'Clark Stephanos', a well-known and beloved man of extreme wealth and influence.

'Look into this man's background,' suggested Lieutenant Baker. 'Rattle all of the cages and see what falls out.'

Just as they were setting out on their assignments, a red-headed clerk of indeterminate age and short stature knocked on the lieutenant's office doorway.

'You wanted information on John Brown and the events at Harper's Ferry, Virginia?' he asked as he was invited into the office.

'Yes, we did,' Doctor Cannon replied. 'What have you got for us?'

'John Brown, a.k.a. Osawatomie Brown,' the researcher told them, 'was an abolitionist who believed that violence was the only way to fight an unholy institution that violated the principles of

Godly Christian standards. On October 17, 1859, he led twenty-one men on a murderous raid on the Federal Arsenal at Harper's Ferry, Virginia.

'Brown's expected uprising of the black slaves and the rallying to his anti-slavery cause failed, and seventeen people died. Brown and his surviving followers of the battle were captured. On December 2, 1859, Brown, after having been tried and convicted, was executed by hanging.

'Over the course of time, his convictions against slavery have been largely forgotten, and his violent methods have been used as a rallying point for extremist groups of varying stripes. He is well-hated, and well-beloved, by people on both sides of many political issues of various times.'

'That seems to be the John Brown Society's manifesto,' Sam concurred. '"Right society's ills through forced and violent change.' No wonder that they would want the super-Taser.'

The team finally broke up, each to pursue his or her own leads. Sam checked Wikipedia for more information about

John Brown, his rabid and radical abolitionist beliefs and methods, and his failed attack on slavery in Virginia before his meeting with Jamie at the bus terminal to compare notes on 'Abel' and his brothers.

Lieutenant Baker gave orders to two detectives to check newspaper and magazine articles for interviews with, and biographical information on, Clark Stephanos.

'Get any background information you can on this man,' he ordered.

Doctor Cannon reviewed the abilities and limitations of the super-Taser and how it interacted with the human body. He was particularly interested in how it was used to kill. *This is the deadliest personal weapon that I have ever seen,* he thought to himself as he studied it.

Jamie used her new clearances to get into encrypted law enforcement files at every level to extract the information she needed on the 'Biblical Brothers'.

'These three brothers have a combined rap sheet a long as Pinocchio's nose,' she told Sam when they sat down at the bus station. 'If 'Cain' and 'Seth' have fixed 'Abel's' death onto us, they won't stop until we, or they, are dead.'

'Mean and vengeful, huh?' was Sam's reply.

'The 'eye for an eye, tooth for a tooth' kind,' Jamie agreed.

They were able to learn that the three brothers had worked as bodyguards and information brokers in Clark Stephanos' enterprises for more than five years. All three of them had been born in the nineteen-nineties to Greek immigrants.

The three boys had been in and out of trouble in the 'Little Sparta' region of a major eastern county city until they had met a fellow Greek who had hired them for various, sometimes illicit, jobs. He had also taught them how to avoid future entanglements with the forces of law and order.

Stephanos himself was believed to be a major player in the actions of several illegal enterprises. No proof was ever substantiated. As his wealth and reputation for altruism grew, so did his political and legal connections. He was implicated in the takeovers, and elimination, of several competitors, but his lawyers and the partners of his legal businesses were always able to provide him with alibis that were iron-clad.

Clark had also cultivated the following of a large number of working-class individuals with whom he had daily contact through generous gifts and attention to their personal lives. Even the legal community was divided as to their feeling toward Clark Stephanos.

There was a fair amount of circumstantial evidence that placed him as one of the kingpins of organized crime in the US and other countries, but there was nothing that a good team of attorneys couldn't have gotten dismissed as hearsay or have made to look like the harassment of an honest and successful citizen by jealous law officials.

His involvement with groups like the Golden BBs was inferred by his early associations with many known, but legally untouchable, members of these groups.

'He has himself well ensconced behind a wall of respectability,' Jamie remarked after two long hours of research on Google, Facebook, Twitter, and other personal information sites. 'Since he has reached the age of majority, his record has been impeccable.'

'A real upright and thoughtful member of society!' was Sam's sarcastic reply. 'Do we know how he was supposed to have attained his wealth and position?'

'Only that he was supposed to have inherited a small company and a few dollars from a grand-uncle. He apparently made wise investments and smart decisions in diversifying his company,' Jamie read. 'Also, he sold a well-managed dot com business just before those kinds of businesses went broke.'

'So now,' Sam frowned, 'he has the perfect way to wash his dirty money and declare taxes on all of his income. Too bad that we can't seem to find someone to testify on how he's been cooking his books.'

★   ★   ★

The Watson families had been enjoying the mild weather at the property where the elder Watson and his wife had been living since his retirement from the UCLA Medical Center in the United States.

'I always wanted to live here where my father grew up,' Doctor Watson remarked as he and his son, the professor, walked the countryside just outside the village. 'There was just something in the way he would reminisce about the moors and other places his grandfather spoke of in his chronicled adventures with his friend, Sherlock Holmes.'

'No doubt,' Professor Watson reflected, 'both he and Sir Conan Doyle used literary license quite a bit.'

'Your great-great-grandfather often admitted to changing, or omitting, certain facts to avoid scandals of one sort or another,' Doctor Watson agreed with his son. 'Even so, many of the cases alluded to are very near actual accounts recorded in the newspapers and historical achieves of the period. While the 221B Baker Street address did not exist at the time, there were several rooming houses and places for rent on the Baker Street of the Victorian era. Any one of those addresses could have been the actual abode of Holmes and Watson.'

'Those are the sorts of details that I wish to use in the doctoral dissertation that I'm researching on my grant. I'd like to be able to leave as complete a record as I can for Jimmy to have as a legacy. I think that Sam would be interested, too,' Professor Watson told his father. 'He seems to be a thoughtful young man, well able to take on his great-grandfather's mantle. According to Jamie, he already has a reputation for astute reasoning and acute observations.'

'According to local legend,' the retired doctor said as he pointed to a group of stones that were perfect for sitting and enjoying the view, 'that is the place where Holmes first met his young wife as an adolescent.'

'The area and the event were described in stories purported to have been the chronicles of her life with Holmes,' the professor told his father. 'Their first meeting was described as a bit adversarial by her.'

'She was described as an intelligent and strong-willed woman by my great-grandfather,' Doctor Watson agreed. 'She was already preparing for her future studies at Oxford University. She was most interested in the history of her mother's people, the Hebrews.

'She was the only survivor of an automobile accident that took the lives of all the other members of her immediate family. When she reached the age of twenty-one, she inherited quite a bit of property on both sides of the Atlantic Ocean. Of course, Mycroft took full advantage of her interest in Palestine to reactivate his brother as one of his agents when the young woman was near the end of her apprenticeship with Sherlock.'

'And the rest,' James remarked, 'as they say, is history.'

As they neared the entrance to the house, Mrs. Watson and Alicia came out to meet them.

'The BBC news just announced an attempted murder as the passengers of the *QE2* disembarked from the ship,' Mrs. Watson told them. 'A woman was wounded and her child was so traumatized that he would not utter any clear words, but just kept screaming! The child's father supposedly showed the port authorities some special papers and got immediate cooperation to lock down the harbor. The woman and child were transported under guard to hospital. The woman had surgery to remove a small-caliber bullet from the area of her rib cage near the place from which she had just transferred her son. No other news has been reported.'

'Oh, James,' Alicia sobbed. 'That could have been me and Jimmy!'

James Watson gathered his wife into his arms and did his best to soothe her.

'Jamie relied well,' Doctor Watson said, his hand on his daughter-in-law's shoulder, 'on her instincts when she learned of those men's intentions. Now we must make plans ourselves. Our enemies may now recognize that they have been tricked.

'Many folks from the village have

grown up on the stories of Holmes, his wife, and their friend, Doctor John H. Watson. They'll be highly motivated to assist us any way that they can.

'When Holmes moved his wife and young son to her properties in the States just before the war, the villagers promised to keep their estates here in good repair and ready for their eventual return, or that of their heirs, should they desire to come home. They've honored that commitment for more that four generations. Let's allow them to decide how they may best assist us at this time. We will not ask them for more than they are able, and willing, to give.

'We will tell them what has happened and let them make their own plans. Our plans will be made according to need and we shall make use of them to strengthen and blend with theirs.'

20

In the hospital, Agent Thorsdatter was resting comfortably after her surgery. Having just shifted the simulacrum from one shoulder to the other had prevented the revelation of their deception.

Agent Roberts was working with the local authorities to get as accurate a picture as possible of the events leading up to the shooting.

'I believe the assassin was trying for a head shot at the child,' he explained after he revealed the previous night's attempt in the infirmary. 'The death of 'little Jimmy' would have wreaked emotional havoc upon all of the Watson family. As the only current member of his generation, he holds a special place in their priorities.'

'There are many citizens of this nation,' said a tall man with a thin face, a long nose, and a habit of running a single finger down the side of it, 'who would do whatever they could to preserve the Holmes and Watson legacy. There are many who owe the advancement and education of their families to Holmes' attentions and training of their forefathers. They are the descendants of the street Arabs that he called his 'Baker Street Irregulars'.'

'There are no doubts in my mind that there were many who were given the chance to become useful citizens,' agreed Roberts graciously. 'If only we had such a group of operatives today. Virtually invisible and totally loyal to their benefactor.'

A man dressed in surgical scrubs walked into the hospital's commissary and asked, 'Which one of you is Agent Roberts?'

'I am,' Roberts identified himself with a slight rising of his hand.

'Your partner is a very fortunate woman,' the surgeon told him in preamble. 'The bullet entered just below the clavicle without hitting any bones. Therefore there was no need to search for bullet fragments or to remove bone splinters.

The bullet also avoided the lung and lodged itself in the muscle and fatty tissues of the left mammary gland.

'We were able to remove the bullet, causing very little additional damage. She'll be very sore, and will need some very powerful pain medication for a while. She should be fully recovered from the anesthesia in the in the next hour or so. I strongly suggest that any visits and questioning be kept to only a few minutes. She will be under sedation as needed for the next forty-eight to seventy-two hours.'

The doctor's report was welcome news to Agent Roberts. After nearly ten years as partners, the two of them had become very close friends.

'Thank you, Doctor,' he said with a sigh of gratitude. 'We've been partners, and friends, a long time.'

The British agent looked at the doctor and asked, 'And how is the 'child'?'

'It has been switched off,' was the answer. 'I understood that you wished to preserve the fiction of its being a living child, so I told everyone that the child had been sedated because of the severe trauma from the sound of the gun and the wounding of his mother. I left orders that only I and a select team of pediatric nurses were to be attending him.'

★ ★ ★

British officers from Scotland Yard were posted outside of Agent Thorsdatter's hospital room, and also posed as pediatric nurses for the 'little Jimmy' simulacrum.

For as long as Thorsdatter was in the hospital, British and American investigators would be busy collecting evidence and having interviews with witnesses. The only conclusions that had been reached were that the weapon had been fired from a building at the medium range for a bullet of that caliber.

At the old bee farm near the southern coast, agents had been sent to act as bodyguards and to keep a watch for unwanted visitors.

'Between the local folk and the official investigators,' Alicia Watson commented, 'we seem to be as well protected as the President or the Prime Minister, and well-informed on the activities of the surrounding countryside.'

'Yes,' her husband agreed, 'it gives me a greater sense of security for your, and Jimmy's, safety. I hope that Jamie and Sam have some luck in shutting down the operations of those two bands of suspects back home. If they can cut off the heads of the vipers after all of us, we'll all feel safer.'

The gentle sounds of the channel and the local fauna gave a pleasant background to the comfortable weather patterns. The property next door to the bee farm, which had belonged to Holmes' wife, had been left to pasture for sheep and cattle. The proceeds received from grazing rights and the sale of honey were placed in a special account at the local bank every quarter. Samuel Holmes could conceivably live comfortably on the interest accumulated from these financial activities. Indeed, the annual income from the sale of his great-grandmother's property in Northern California had made it possible for him to purchase a comfortable home in London, California after his parents had died. His great-grandfather had passed away before he could return to his home in England at the end of the war. His great-grandmother had stayed in the United States until her son was grown, deeding her property to him when she returned to the country that had given birth to her mother and her husband. There she lived quietly until her death, returning periodically to visit her son and grandson.

After her death, her grandson had made the current financial arrangements with the bank and the villagers for the care and disbursement of funds from the combined properties of his grandparents. His will had left everything to his son, Samuel, and any future progeny.

The combined incomes from the English properties of his great-grandparents were held in trust until Sam, or one of his heirs, should decide to claim them.

'So,' Doctor Watson proclaimed as they discussed these matters after dinner one night, 'Sam is the heir that no one has ever seen? Between both incomes, he could live comfortably for the rest of his life without having to work, and probably never having to touch the principal of either source. That's just as well, knowing the hazards of his current chosen profession. His ancestors would have approved of his work ethic.

'Of course, we Watsons are far from being paupers ourselves. Doctor John H. Watson invested his writing income well, and also instilled a sense of *noblesse oblige* in his descendants.'

Jimmy, who had recovered quickly from his jet lag, was ready for his routine game of 'Chutes and Ladders' with the adults before getting ready for bed. He had waited until his parents and grandparents had begun to clear the used dishes from the table before asking to be excused. He then went to where the boxes of board games were kept and got the box of his favorite game.

'Grandpa tell story before bedtime?' he inquired hopefully.

'Okay, Jimmy,' Doctor Watson agreed. 'This is a story that my grandpa told me when I was little. It's called 'The Final Problem'.'

21

'Jamie,' Sam's voice revealed his angry frustration as he threw his empty cup in the trash, 'I know that the law says that all juvenile records are sealed by the courts once a person reaches voting age, but there must be a way to look into them, or maybe get a judge to let us have a look at the records that are related to a particular case! Surely the law allows for extenuating circumstances on a need-to-know basis.'

'You know that that law was made so that young people who had made mistakes based upon bad choices could have clean records when they began their adult careers,' Jamie retorted. 'The incorrigible may use what they've learned to keep from being hounded by the authorities, but many take their second chance at respectability to truly turn their lives around and enter careers that would have been denied them otherwise.'

'I know the law was meant to help kids who really wish to change,' Sam was still frustrated, 'but it also hampers law enforcement efforts as often as not. I really wish that I could see Clark in person. There's something familiar about him.'

'The online version of the LonCal *Times* says that Mr. Stephanos is giving an after-luncheon speech on Thursday at the fund raiser for a new park to be built in the older section of the city. I'll see if there are any open seats for the lunch. We'll get to see and hear him then. Maybe things will click together for you.'

'All right.' Sam was not completely mollified, but took Jamies' offering with good grace. 'Let's see how far back we can find pictures of him. Maybe I'll recognize something from them.'

★   ★   ★

Thursday found Sam and Jamie at the luncheon as guests of the city and as added security. Clark Stephanos rose from his chair after having been introduced by the head of the Parks and Recreations Department.

'I would like to begin today by saying that I'm glad to be here today. It isn't just any country where a person with humble beginnings can rise, through hard work and ingenuity, to a place of prominence such as I have achieved. Every child deserves a safe place to interact with his peers and become the best person that he or she can be. I hereby pledge to match all donations, up to a hundred thousand dollars. It is my hope that our children may avoid many of the pitfalls that befell many of my generation.'

Clark's speech continued for another five to ten minutes, extolling the hopes and dreams that could shape the younger generation if given the proper environment.

As Jamie was leaving with the crowd, she observed Sam converse with Clark for a few moments, and then shake his hand before rejoining her.

'Did you notice the small scar on Clark's jaw, just below his right ear?' he questioned as he took her hand in the crook of his elbow. 'It's not very noticeable and doesn't show up very well in his photographs. I knew of an older boy when I went to school in the City of Jurupa Valley who had been injured in a gang fight. He got sliced by a knife and had also received a bullet wound in his left leg. Later, one of the rival gang members was found with a broken neck and wounds that matched the other boy's. No one was arrested for the killing, even though circumstantial evidence pointed to the kid with the knife and bullet wounds. The two gangs were watched for a long time, and their activities eventually settled down.'

'When we get back to your house,' Jamie told him, 'why don't we check the online archives of the local paper. Do you remember about when this happened?'

'I think it was the summer after I had finished middle school,' he said after searching his memory. 'That would be about ten years or twelve ago. The paper had already begun to save their articles electronically by then, I think.'

Now that Sam had seen, heard, and talked with Clark Stephanos, he remembered that several members of the cliques at the high school had attempted to get him to join their 'clubs' when he was a freshman.

He had been too independently-minded to even give most of them a second thought. When several boys attempted to 'persuade' him to become one of their members, his training in baritsu soon made them decide to leave him alone. The lightning moves of his fighting techniques led to continuing entreaties for him to teach them to other high school students. He always told them that he was not a master of any martial art form, and therefore was not qualified to teach. One of the most persistent persons was no longer a student, but a very early graduate with a horse face and cold eyes.

Sam remembered having taken an active dislike to the young man. He had heard that this young, intelligent tough had been alleged to have been the warlord for one of the two gangs that had caused such a major crisis during the summer before he had started high school. His intelligence had been recognized by his finishing the four-year course in just a little over two years.

Sam, already showing a high degree of interest in criminology and an innate skill at observation along with a gift for thinking 'outside the box', was eventually able to lead his police mentors to clues that put the young man in Juvenile Hall until his eighteenth birthday.

Sam's testimony and evidence gathering had caused his adversary to promise retribution in the future. Since Sam had heard nothing from, or about, the man after his release, he assumed that his enemy had forgotten him.

'Mr. Stephanos' career seems to have begun only about eight years ago,' Jamie told Sam as she read the biography from Wikipedia on her laptop at Sam's kitchen table. 'He arrived in London with a small start-up fund. After three years, he had amassed nearly a million dollars in capital and had acquired a group of properties that added up to several million dollars in value. His current net worth is estimated to be between a billion and billion and a half dollars. His charitable donations would be enough to buy a small company outright.

'No one knows anything of his past previous to his coming to our fair city, but his actions and citizenship since then have been exemplary.'

Sam looked up from his desktop computer at his nearby desk and observed, 'The timing would be right. I found the article about the gang war that summer I spoke of. Listen.'

He read the news article that had described the horrifying and bloody activities that had led to several deaths of highly-placed members of both gangs. Police and Sheriff's officers had been able to arrest, and have tried as adults, many of the members of both gangs, and had finally been able to bring down the levels of violence and reprisal in the area. In a follow-up piece, there was a picture of the young man who had been injured in the bloodiest battle between the two gangs.

"'Also being sought as a person of interest',' Sam read, "'is Stephen Clark, sixteen, in the death of Leon Mylar, the number-two man of the 'Black Knights'. Clark is thought to be the number-three man, and warlord, of the 'Hand of Fate'. No evidence is forthcoming to arrest Clark on any of a number of suspected crimes.'

'This is definitely a picture of our 'Clark Stephanos'. He is also the one that my testimony had sent to that underage prison about eleven years ago. Now I at least know why he wants revenge on me. Why he does he want you and your family? That's what I can't figure out.'

Jamie had no answer either, so she returned to her research.

Two hours later, the tune of 'Flight of the Bumblebee' played on Jamie's cellphone.

'Doctor Watson,' she said when she had opened the connection.

'This is Lieutenant Baker at headquarters,' came the answering voice. 'Is Sergeant Holmes with you?'

'We're in his kitchen,' Jamie told him,

her curiosity aroused. 'What's happening?'

'You remember our favorite tabloid reporter from the *Midnight Confessor*?'

'Yes, what about him?'

'He's in the hospital.' Lieutenant Baker's voice was grim. 'Apparently, a hit-and-run driver didn't care for the way he crossed the street. The doctors say that he'll pull through, but that he's going to have a long, hard recovery period.'

Jamie told Sam what she had just been told.

'Are we needed?' Sam inquired with a look of concern on his face. 'Does he want to speak with either of us?'

Jamie repeated Sam's question to Lieutenant Baker, and was told that, even though R.R. had asked for them, the doctors had put him under heavy pain medication. Several hours would be needed before he would be coherent enough to answer questions or have visitors.

Jamie disconnected after Lieutenant Baker had promised to call if anything changed.

'Things are happening fast.' She looked

across the kitchen at Sam. 'First, James and Alicia's decoys have their room aboard ship set on fire, then they are shot at; and now our star slimeball is hit by a car, apparently on his way to the station to give us some information. As an FME, I'm not used to this intense level of personal involvement.'

'And with three different government agencies involved just in our own country, it doesn't look like it will get any better until this case is solved,' Sam replied as he made a new pot of coffee. 'This connection to my own past needs to be looked into. I wonder if Sergeant Valdez or any of his contemporaries are still around.'

A check with the Jurupa Valley police department gave them the information they needed on Esteban Valdez, now a retired captain; and, after a few minutes of catching up, arrangements were made to meet at the city's local Denny's late the next morning.

★   ★   ★

'The city sure has changed since I went to school here,' Sam remarked after he and Jamie had been shown to the table where Valdez, still fit and muscular, was waiting for them. 'I saw two new shopping centers as I drove down Mission Boulevard. The city has a cleaner, more modern look.'

''Your tax dollars at work',' Valdez remarked. 'It took a few years to get through the early growing pains, but the council and the residents have really put things together in the last five years or so. They even convinced the state people to return the start-up funds that they had kept from us.'

The waitress delivered their coffee and left them to their conversation.

'Yeah,' Valdez sighed as the waitress left, 'Stephen Clark was a real piece of work. Until you gathered the evidence that convicted him of felony theft and burglary, he was always able to talk his way out of all but a couple of infractions and misdemeanors. Even Clark's lawyers couldn't disprove your evidence or shake your testimony. That was detective work as good as any I've ever seen. And you were only a second-year Youth Auxiliary!'

'He hasn't changed, sir,' Sam said as he began to report on the events of the past month. 'He's changed his name to Clark Stephanos, and runs several profitable and legitimate businesses.

'A lot of folks believe that he is a well-intentioned philanthropist and that he is charitable to many of the working people that he comes into daily contact with. However, the FBI and Military Intelligence have photos tying him in with a gun-running terrorist organization known as the Golden BBs. Right now, there's not enough hard evidence to make an arrest, or to get a conviction.

'A man from a very black government ops group who has a man inside the BBs gave us the information that Jamie, her entire family, and I are on their 'Most Wanted Dead' list. An attempt on Jamie's nephew was foiled by using FBI decoy agents and a computer-controlled facsimile.

'Yesterday, Stephanos gave an after-luncheon speech that Jamie and I were able to attend. After having heard him speak and seen him in person, I was certain that Stephen Clark and Clark Stephanos were the same person. After lunch, I had the opportunity to speak with him for a few minutes about one of his remarks, and to look closely at his face as he answered my question. By the time we shook hands and parted, I knew beyond any doubt that he was the same person that I knew when I lived here.'

'Do you have anything else to go on?' Valdez questioned. 'Do you have a chain of evidence yet?'

'Currently,' Jamie stated for the both of them, 'all we have is conjecture and circumstantial evidence. We believe that we have enough to lead us to more substantial efforts for our lines of inquiries.'

'Put your case together solidly, and don't be afraid of conflicting evidence trails,' the retired captain advised them. 'When you know you've got your perp, find that one irrefutable piece of evidence and nail your suspect to the wall.'

'And always remember that the burden

of proof,' Sam added, 'lies with the prosecution.'

'I see,' Valdez chuckled, 'that you haven't forgotten your lessons!'

The three detectives discussed at length the history of Stephen Clark, a.k.a. Clark Stephanos. All agreed that Clark was, indeed, their most likely suspect, especially when his history was factored into the equation.

Even though the evidence was still shaky, recent events had made Sam even surer that his quarry was near to being caught in his own trap. Like Professor Moriarty, Clark seemed determined to bring down his old nemesis, even if it meant his own destruction.

★　★　★

'As a gang warlord,' Sam reflected during their drive back to London, 'Clark must have planned a lot of the battles against the Black Knights. That means that he is used to planning in detail.'

'Someone who is always looking ahead several moves and making plans for when things go awry,' Jamie added. 'That's not someone you want for an enemy.'

'Especially if he has learned the lesson of delayed gratification.' Sam's face was devoid of emotions as he drove his car along the interstate. 'If the eyes are the windows to the soul, then his soul is not only corrupt, but dead. I don't look forward to our final meeting.'

'I would have to agree with that assessment.' Jamie looked at Sam, trying to get some indication from his body language as to his state of mind. 'A man who's as cold as Al Capone, and can imitate an Albert Schweitzer, is a *very* scary person.'

They continued the rest of their ride home in silence.

When Sam finally arrived at Jamie's apartment, he carefully checked the surroundings before walking his partner to her door.

Jamie unlocked her door and allowed Sam to enter first. Not having found any apparent signs of intruders, Sam stepped into the hallway, allowing Jamie room to enter.

'No surprises this time,' he said as Jamie walked past him into the living area. 'I'll check the rest of the apartment before I go home.'

'Would you like some coffee before you leave?' Jamie asked Sam when he had finished his inspection.

'It's been a long day,' he responded, 'and a long drive as well. I think I'd better take a rain check on the coffee and get home.'

Jamie reached out and lightly touched Sam's cheek before he turned toward the door.

'Be careful, Sam,' she said as she watched him walk down the sidewalk.

As Sam walked to his car, he puzzled over what had just transpired. Was their involvement heading beyond professionalism? If so, how far was he prepared to go? How far was she?

Sam checked his voice-mail as soon as he got in his door. SAC Jones had left a medical update about Agent Thorsdatter's condition.

'She's recovering nicely,' he reported. 'The British authorities have found the weapon that was used in the building that the bullet's trajectory indicated.

'If Thorsdatter had been wearing a vest, she wouldn't have been wounded by the .25 caliber rifle. The shot was definitely intended for the child. Security has been stepped up at the hospital and at the bee farm where the Watsons are staying.

'James's father has enlisted the aid of several villagers in an effort to apprehend the assassin.

'Needless to say, British Customs and Scotland Yard are livid thinking about how anyone could get an unauthorized firearm into the country. I think that eventually, there'll be some resignations and/or firings of personnel.

'I'll call again as more news becomes available.'

Sam called Jamie, relayed Jones's message, and then went to bed.

The next morning turned out to be a dark, dreary day. The sky was filled with rain clouds.

As Sam finished his second cup of coffee and his breakfast, his phone rang.

'Sam!' Jamie said excitedly as soon as

she heard his voice. 'Turn on CNN. You've got to see this!'

Sam quickly switched on his television and tuned in to CNN. The news commentator was reading a report.

'British authorities have reportedly arrested a man believed to have attempted the assassination of US FBI agent Sarah Thorsdatter. Thorsdatter was part of a decoy team being used to protect a US university professor and his family on sabbatical to London and Southern England gathering information on his doctorial dissertation about nineteenth-century English history.

'The professor and his family are staying with his parents, a retired medical doctor from the UCLA Medical Center and his wife, at their home on the Southern Coast.

'The alleged shooter had apparently discovered the FBI's ruse and was captured when neighbors reported a suspicious person attempting to approach the house located on an old bee farm.

'The two academics, along with a Mr. Sonderson, the conservator of the bee farm and the adjacent property, were able to keep the suspect under surveillance until the local constabulary could arrive.

'As they waited for the authorities to arrive, the suspect was observed opening a long case and removing what appeared to be a rifle with night scope.

'When the person was seen to aim the weapon at the kitchen window, the doctor shouted a warning at the house, startling the suspect as he fired his weapon. The bullet went through the upper portion of the kitchen window and lodged in the opposite wall.

'The doctor, professor, and Mr. Sonderson, who is a retired member of Scotland Yard, subdued the man and held him for the village police, who had arrived in time to witness the shooting.

'The suspect was taken into custody. Early ballistics reports indicate that the weapon was of a similar type used, and found, at the *QE2* shooting.'

Sam switched off his TV and spoke into the phone.

'Jamie?' Sam was concerned for Jamie's emotional state. 'Are you okay? Have you heard anything from your dad or your brother?'

'No,' said a worried Jamie. 'And I can't get through to England on either my cellphone or my regular phone. There's no way to communicate with them!'

'Okay, Jamie,' Sam was trying to stay calm for Jamie's sake, 'we'll get in touch with them somehow, or they'll contact us. I'll be there as quickly as I can.'

Sam rushed out to his car, preparing to drive to Jamie's apartment. He dropped his keys in his haste to unlock the car door. As he stooped to pick them up, there was a loud pop, and the driver's door window of his car shattered explosively.

Sam fell flat on the pavement as he unholstered his pistol and looked for any sign of the shooter.

'This is starting to annoy me,' Sam said out loud to himself.

Off in the distance, Sam heard the wail of sirens coming closer.

One of the neighbors must have heard the shot and called 911, he thought as he cautiously stood back up. *Maybe we can find out something that can be of use this time.*

Sam reholstered his gun and pulled out his detective ID. He waited for the uniformed officers to arrive.

The first officers to arrive on the scene were a man and a woman who had been patrol officers in his neighborhood for about three years.

'Hey, Roger; hey, Cheryl,' he greeted them as they pulled up next to the curb in front of his house. 'I'm glad that you were close by. If I hadn't been in a hurry and dropped my keys, I'd still be on the street.'

'This is, what, the third time you've been involved with someone wanting to do away with you?' Cheryl asked him.

'Yeah, Sarge,' Roger teased. 'I'm beginning to think that someone really dislikes you!'

'Listen, guys.' Sam's look was serious enough to get their attention. 'I really need to contact Doctor Watson and let her know what's going on here, and to have an officer be with her.'

'I'll call in the request, Roger,' Cheryl said as she got on the radio. 'You get

Sam's statement and any other information he remembers.'

While she was on the radio, Detectives Johns and Smyth arrived and walked over to where Sam was giving his statement to Roger.

After a few jesting remarks regarding Sam's magnetic attraction to bullets, everyone got down to the serious business of evidence gathering. Other uniforms searched the area for a bullet casing or any other evidence left by the perpetrator as they waited for Sam to leave his house.

Behind a tall hedge along the border of the empty property across the street, other officers found imprints in the ground, damp from the late-night rain, which seemed to indicate that a person had been standing there for some time. There was also another, differently-shaped imprint, that could have been the mark a rifle butt had made as it rested upon the ground.

A sharp-eyed patrolwoman, making a thorough search of the hedge, found a brass shell casing in the dirt underneath the branches.

'Our perp seems to have made his exit in a hurry after he missed you,' Smyth commented when the officers told him what they'd found. 'And after waiting so patiently for Sergeant Holmes to come outside, too.'

While the evidence team was making a complete search of the yard and surrounding area where the shell casing had been found, the investigating team canvassed the neighborhood for anyone who had seen or heard anything out of the ordinary at the empty property. The only person who admitted to seeing anything was a woman who had nearly been knocked down by a young man running down the street, who had got into a blue Chevrolet Malibu that had needed a wash very badly. The car was so dirty that the license plate's numbers and letters were obscured, and the windows so filthy that she remembered wondering how anyone could see out of them to drive.

While Sam was still giving his report to Johns and Smyth, an unmarked police cruiser pulled up out in front of Sam's house and double-parked next to the detectives' car. The front passenger door opened and a very worried-looking Jamie stepped out.

'I can't leave you alone for ten minutes,' she tried to cover her concern with humor, 'without you upsetting the other boys. Can't you learn to play nice?'

'Aw, Mom,' Sam replied in the same lighthearted manner. 'They won't let me play, and when I try to take my bat and ball and go home, they get mad!'

'Little Jimmy would never forgive you if you got yourself killed!' Jamie's tone was now one of anger. 'He was really taken with you, you know.'

'I didn't ask to be shot at!' Sam's face was beginning to turn red from his own rising anger at her remarks. 'These assassins keep coming out of the ground like those dragon's teeth soldiers from that Greek myth!'

'You two can finish your lovers' quarrel *after* we complete our preliminary investigation,' Smyth said, with mild pique in his voice. 'Sergeant Holmes is obviously on someone's hit parade, and the sooner we can put this person away, the sooner the two of you can go about your own investigation without all of these interruptions.'

Jamie and Sam gave each other a look of chagrin, and then smiled.

'That's better,' Detective Smyth said, giving each of them a firm look. 'Now, Sergeant Holmes, you said that you were headed to your car, planning to go to Jamie's apartment after she had called you. Would you tell me why?'

'There had been a disturbing new report on CNN about a certain event in Southern England that had her upset. She hadn't been able to contact any of her family members in the UK to verify that they were unhurt by the event. I was going over to her place to help her to get more information. I dropped my car keys, and when I bent to pick them up, a shot went over my head and through the car window.'

'Were you able to get a look at the shooter?'

'No. But the hedge at the house across the street rustled, and I saw a section sway as if someone had backed away from it and had caught, or pulled, something in the branches. I didn't notice anything else.'

'The hedge is pretty overgrown all the way around the property,' Johns observed. 'That would have kept him from being observed. The officers did find a place where some branches had been broken as if by someone forcing their way through.'

Questions were asked in half a dozen different ways or more, trying to get Sam to remember anything at all about the attempt on his life. After an hour, everyone thought that they had as much information as they could get for the moment.

As they were leaving, the radio in Johns' and Smyth's cruiser demanded attention. Smyth answered the call and, after listening for a minute or two, he got out and walked back to Sam and Jamie, who were still standing by his front door.

'The blue Chevy Malibu was found in a long-term paid parking lot,' Smyth told them. 'After the license plate had been made readable and the numbers checked, the car was found to have been left there some time ago, and had been reported stolen. It looks as if our perp was waiting for an opportunity to take you out, Sam. Whatever you two are working on has stirred up a nest of very angry hornets.'

22

At the old bee farm in England, a recently released Agent Thorsdatter and her partner, Agent Roberts, were sitting in the living room with all of the adult Watsons.

Since the youngest Watson was in his bed asleep, they spoke very quietly.

'The man who took a shot at your kitchen window has been put on suicide watch,' Roberts told the others. 'The locals and Scotland Yard all feel that he may be inclined to attempt drastic measures rather than take the chance that he may reveal information that his employers don't want known.'

'From what Sam and Jamie told us back in Nevada,' James Watson commented, 'that may be the lesser of two evils in his mind. These people are unforgiving and don't allow for unforeseen situations. You either succeed or you don't get a second chance.'

'Scotland Yard is convinced that he is the same man that took a shot at Sarah as she got off the boat holding the simulacrum?' Doctor Watson asked.

'He was using the same type and caliber of rifle as the one found at the harbor landing,' Thorsdatter replied. 'They haven't got all of the ballistic and other forensic reports back on the two weapons used in the shootings, but they're fairly certain that both were done by the same person. They definitely have him as possessing an illegal firearm that had been used in a crime. Scotland Yard is looking for any evidence pointing to other criminal activities in this country by this person.'

'I wonder if telling him that he's free to go because there's not enough evidence to hold him any longer would get him to tell them anything,' Alicia considered out loud. 'If he's afraid of his employers, he might feel safer in jail.'

'The way I understand it,' Agent Roberts told her, 'Scotland Yard doesn't believe that would work. They think that he has been conditioned to believe that his life is already forfeit because of his failure and that he is honor-bound to take his own life.'

'Then, we'll just have to find some other way to get him to tell what he knows,' Mary Watson stated firmly. 'I believe in the power of persuasion. Of course one must find the right leverage.'

They all agreed that they needed a very strong and very convincing argument to get the information that they needed, but they were at a loss as to what that argument might be.

The next day, as Caleb Roberts and Sarah Thorsdatter were waiting at the clinic to have Sarah's wound dressing changed, Caleb remarked, 'Mary and Alicia are very perceptive and opinionated women.'

'Yes, they did have some definite ideas about how our suspect should be handled,' Sarah replied. 'I have the suspicion that Alicia would rather employ the same method that a mother bear would use defending her only cub.'

'And what might that be, Sarah?'

'Rip him up until he no longer has any

interest in her offspring.'

'Then I think that it's a good thing that she's calm enough to realize that the real threat is his bosses. We really need to pin them down somehow.'

The doctor came out and called Sarah's name and she went in to have her dressing changed and her wound checked.

'You're healing nicely,' the doctor said as she applied the clean dressing. 'The reports from Emergency said that the bullet missed the bones and blood vessels. No collateral damage to the surrounding tissues caused by bullet or bone fragmentation. Do you have any unusual weakness or numbness on that side of your body?'

'No,' Sarah answered. 'I took some shrapnel from a ricochet a few years ago, so I know that you're concerned about possible nerve damage, but I don't feel anything out of the ordinary for having a bullet wound.'

'Good,' the doctor said. 'We'll still need to run some tests in a few days just in case so we can be sure.'

As Sarah left the examination room, she was thinking about how fortunate it was that she was left-handed. She had been carrying the toddler-sim on her right shoulder, and had just shifted the weight to her left when the shot was fired. She knew a lot of nerves for the muscles of the shoulder and arm were near the entry wound. No matter how careful the doctors had been when they extracted the bullet, permanent damage to those nerves could have been done inadvertently.

'The doctor was pretty positive about the way I seem to be healing,' she told Caleb as she met him in the waiting room. 'She wants to run a few tests later to be sure there isn't something that they missed, just as a routine follow-up.'

'Good,' Caleb responded as they left the clinic and returned to their hotel.

★　★　★

The next day at the bee farm was chilly but clear after the early-morning fog burned off. Little Jimmy was having fun chasing some kittens as they romped through the yard surrounding the house.

His birthday party three days earlier had been fun and exciting. Several of the village children had attended and he had enjoyed having so many new friends. His grandmother had made his birthday cake, decorating it with Papa Smurf and other favorite cartoon characters.

As one of the kittens pounced upon a butterfly, Jimmy heard the sound of a car coming up the driveway to the house. Wondering who was visiting, he went back into the house.

Inside, he saw a stranger in his grandmother's kitchen.

The man seemed to make his grandmother nervous, and that made Jimmy scared. He stayed out of sight and watched the man.

'Tell your daughter,' he said, 'that if she doesn't want anyone else hurt, she and her boyfriend will drop their investigation and forget all they've learned.'

The man turned, went out of the house, and got into the car he had parked outside. As he was leaving, he passed

Jonathan and James Watson as they returned from the village.

'I wonder who that was?' Doctor Watson asked himself aloud as he continued on up to the house.

As he neared the house, he and James saw Jimmy on the porch with his grandmother holding onto him tightly. Jimmy was in tears, even though he was trying to act brave.

'What's wrong, Mary?' Jonathan inquired as he quickly made his way onto the porch. 'Why is Jimmy crying?'

'Bad man come and scare Grandma and Jimmy!' Jimmy sobbed. 'He said he wants to hurt Auntie Jamie and Sam.'

Jonathan quickly dialed the village constabulary and then his friend, Joe Sonderson.

He gave a description of the car to the police and told Joe that he wanted someone to watch Mary, Alicia, and Jimmy.

'Where's Alicia?' James wished to know.

'She went over to the pasture to check on that cow that's about ready to drop her calf,' Mary told her son. 'She said that she wanted to bring her up near the house in case she was ready to deliver.'

'Do you know where the cattle are?' her husband asked with a worried look on his face.

'Over by the brook where the stiles are, to keep them from getting bogged down in the mud.'

'I'm going to go look for her,' James told his parents. 'Will you look after Jimmy for me?'

'Of course we will, Son,' Jonathan told him. 'Joe should be here any minute. He can help you look for Alicia. He can help, too, if she needs assistance with that pregnant cow. They can be stubborn sometimes when they're about to drop a calf.'

Even though he wanted to rush out and find his wife, James saw the wisdom of having the other man along. Not only could he be of aid if another's strength was necessary, but he also knew the lie of the land better.

After an hour of searching, James and Sonderson found Alicia near the brook where Mary Watson had told them that the cattle were to be found that day. They had missed her at first because she had been down in a gully. The cow had wandered down the slope and been unable to climb back out.

'I was just about to call you on your cell,' Alicia told them when she saw Joe and her husband. 'That stupid cow is too heavy to climb out of this gulley on her own, and I've been trying to help her, but I can't get enough leverage to push her up the slope.'

'Okay, Mrs. Watson,' Joe said, as relieved as James to find her unharmed. 'You take this lead rope after I put it on her, and pull while your husband and I push her from behind. The three of us should be able to get her back up the slope.'

The two men and the woman were finally able to get the cow back up out of the gulley and up on level ground.

'Good thing we found you,' James said. 'She would never have made it out by herself, even with you helping her.'

After Joe checked the cow over for injuries, he told the Watsons that he thought that she should be taken to the calving barn.

'She'll most likely have her calf by tomorrow morning,' he let them know. 'This one had twins the last time she dropped. She looks big enough to do it again. You were right to want her up near the house, Missus.'

James decided to wait until they had the cow put away in the barn before he told his wife about the visitor they'd had that morning.

When Alicia was finally told, she barely controlled her feelings of hysteria.

'How do these people keep getting past all of the security on us?' she wanted to know.

'The inspector on this case believes that they may have someone on the inside,' Joe replied with a downcast face. 'Too much information seems to be known for things to be otherwise.'

The evening passed quietly enough — until after supper, when shouts of surprise and pain were heard from near the barn where several of the beehives were kept. There were also sounds from the cow that indicated she was going into labor.

'Jonathan,' said Joe, who was spending the night, 'is your pistol loaded?'

'Only with rat shot,' he replied. 'That's the only way I could get a permit.'

'Grab it and follow me!'

Joe put on his coat and checked the service revolver he had in his pocket. 'I always kept my license up to date after my retirement from the Yard,' he remarked as Jonathan came down from the bedroom with his pistol in his hand.

Quietly, the two men crept out of the house by the back door. On the ground, they saw a man with his hands and arms slapping at several angry bees that were stinging him.

'You go check on the cow while I get the bee repellent and get them away from the man on the ground,' Jonathan told Joe. 'I don't think he's in any shape to be a threat.'

Joe stooped over and, using his forefinger and his thumb, carefully picked up a rifle with a sniper scope.

'I think the coppers will want to see this,' he said as he walked into the barn.

The bees were forced to retreat, and

Doctor Watson led the stranger into the house.

'You're fortunate that we were home, young man,' he told his patient, as he placed salve on the bee stings. 'Anyone who approaches too close to the hives of this particular breed of bees without the proper scent is attacked as a threat.'

'Those bees are killers!' the stranger said. 'You should be locked up and those bees destroyed!'

'Now, just calm down, young man,' Jonathan told him. 'I'm sure that the police will want to know what you were doing on private property with a loaded weapon that was configured for night-time assassination. Especially after a previous attempt has been made upon members of this family, and a man was here this afternoon making threats on my daughter and her partner back in the States. By the way, the man out in the barn is a retired Scotland Yard Inspector. He's good at preserving evidence.'

The police arrived soon after the stranger had had his bee stings attended to. After taking Watson's and Sonderson's statements, they took the man to the village jail, and received the rifle as evidence.

'These rifles must have been bought wholesale,' one of the officers said after looking at it. 'This is the third one we've found since those FBI blokes were shot at. Two were apparently going to be used by intruders on your property, Doctor.'

'Yes,' the younger Watson said. 'We reported a stranger who came here making threats. And now this fellow shows up. Little Jimmy's really scared.'

Just then, the cow in the barn bawled for attention.

'I think we'd better check on Bossy,' Joe told everyone. 'That sounded like she's ready.'

The officers left with their prisoner. Joe and all of the Watsons went into the barn.

'We help Bossy have her baby?' Jimmy asked excitedly. 'How does she know what to do?'

'The good Lord has given all animals what are called 'instincts', Jimmy,' his grandmother told him. 'That tells them what they need to know about a lot of things. They only need human help if things aren't working the way they should. Humans have other mothers and doctors to tell them what to do and to help them. Besides, Bossy had twins nearly two years ago, so she knows from experience what she needs to do.'

Jimmy had a lot of questions as the labor progressed. Finally, around midnight, Bossy's calf was born. Jimmy was amazed at how quickly the calf was standing and nursing. With a yawn, he commented on how much work mothers had to do to have their babies.

'Yes, they do,' Alicia told him. 'Bossy and her baby will need to sleep soon, and I think that the rest of us should get some sleep now, too.'

23

The reports from England had just arrived at Lieutenant Baker's desk just as Sam and Jamie had settled in to begin their workday. As soon as he had read the report, the lieutenant sent word for them to join him in his office.

'The latest word from England says that another attempt at the Watsons' bee farm was foiled when he approached too close to some of the hives and the bees attacked him,' Baker explained. 'The man was taken to the medical ward of the prison after Doctor Watson treated him for multiple bee stings. Apparently, he had in his possession the same type of weapon used in the previous attempt, and which was also used in the attack on Agents Roberts and Thorsdatter.'

'I think we have enough information to do a little snooping at the places we know that Clark frequents,' Jamie said with a studied look on her face. 'We can't pin any illegal activities on his part, but maybe we can catch one of his assistants in an act of impropriety.'

'And I think I know just the person to follow up on.' Sam was in agreement. 'But first, we have a hospital visit to make.'

'R.R.'s been cleared to have visitors?' Jamie wished to know.

'That's right,' Lieutenant Baker told them. 'I got the word that he was asking to see the two of you just before I asked you into my office. It seems that he was quite insistent.'

'That'll save us some time trying to get in to see him.' Sam was grateful that R.R. was doing well enough to be asking for them.

'Scum of the earth he may be,' Jamie commented, 'but he's *our* scum, and deserves our protection and attention.'

Half an hour later, Jamie and Sam were in R.R.'s hospital room. Fortunately, R.R. had been able to dodge the hit-and-run driver fast enough that he had avoided crippling or life-threatening injuries.

'I saw the car deliberately swerve

toward me,' R.R. informed them. 'I think that the BBs and the John Brown Society believe I may have found out sumthin' about their activities. Thinkin' back on ever'thin', mebbe I have.' R.R.'s eyes closed in thought for moment. 'Yeah, I do know sumthin'. Those guys that Doctor Watson calls th' Biblical Brothers? They're old-time members of a gang of Greek Warrior wannabes that called themselves the CCCs. They operated outta th' Little Sparta zone near the eastern border of the county. I'm told that the gang got absorbed by an outta-towner claimin' to be a Greek immigrant and his business partners. No one knows exactly who he and the partners are, or where they came from, but a lotta the gang bangers suddenly went legit and appear to have stayed clean as far as the law goes. The Gang Information Center hasn't had any hard evidence on 'em for a coupl'a years or so.

'O' course, the brothers keep showin' up on th' cops' radar, but now that 'Abel' has showed up mortally wounded after that shootout, they know that 'Seth' and 'Cain' ain't th' lily-whites they pretend ta be.'

'Is there reason to believe that they're connected to the John Brown Society?' Sam was trying to put the pieces of the puzzle together. 'Their stated manifesto doesn't seem to accurately mesh together with the BBs' agenda very smoothly.' In Sam's mind, the militia wannabes were an ill-fitting cog in the smooth-running machinery of the BBs' endeavors. 'All of our knowledge of the J.B. Society would indicate that the group is a red herring.'

'They do act like a stalking horse, don't they?' Jamie interjected. 'They keep up just enough activity to draw our attention. I can't find anything about them before the leaks about, and the thefts of, the super-Tasers.

'My sources tell me,' R.R. spoke up, 'that they didn't even exist before a few months ago.'

'So,' Sam turned thoughtful, 'instead of a legitimate company to laundry their dirty money, Clark and his associates have created a group that can be blamed and used as fall guys for their illegal purposes. A cover for their operations that can be used to distract us from their real goals. Clark really does see himself as a spider of crime. He controls all of the threads of his web from one source, and weaves the traps of his intricate empire from his throne room.'

'This 'Clark' you mentioned,' R.R. asked as he used the remote to adjust his hospital bed to a more comfortable position, 'you sound as if you know him.'

'He and I have clashed before,' Sam replied. 'Back in my early high-school days. He assumed that he was invulnerable. I proved that assumption to be invalid. He was sent to Juvenile Detention until he was eighteen. Now he seems to be looking for a magic bullet to bring me down.'

★   ★   ★

Sam and Jamie drove to the City Hall's Records Building, intending to do a search of Clark Stephanos' business activities. They looked up the dates that each of his businesses began operation or were purchased.

'There's a pattern beginning to take place here,' Jamie said as she placed the information into a spreadsheet using date, type, and place of each start-up or acquisition. 'Most of the acquisitions seem to have been made after the owner's death, retirement, or bankruptcy. The start-ups were all made just as new technologies or production techniques were being tested.'

'Insider information,' Sam commented thoughtfully, 'or perhaps the use of forceful persuasion to let him have rights to patents he didn't own? That sounds like the tactics that Stephen Clark was using when I helped put him away all those years ago. He was not just the warlord for the Hand of Fate, he worked to make the gang into a profitable, if illegal, business venture. The gang's strong-arm tactics forced several small businesses to grant them controlling interests. That was the evidence I used to send him to detention. Not even the best lawyers that he could hire were able to get him or his confederates off. He was the only one that was tried as a juvenile. The others were all tried, and convicted as adults and got corresponding sentences. One or two are still in prison.'

'Do you think that they might be willing to talk about Clark after all this time?' Jamie asked out of curiosity. 'After all, they're serving sentences as adults and Clark only did time until he legally became an adult and was freed. Do you think that they might want a little payback?'

'A lot would depend on any bargains Clark made with them,' Sam said after thinking for a moment. 'If Clark offered the right inducements for their silence, revenge may not be on their minds.'

'If that's true,' Jamie responded, 'then we'll have to come up with an offer that is too good to refuse.'

'Yeah, but what have we got to offer?'

'We'll just have to think of something.'

After taking a break for lunch, they went to the courthouse to get permission to speak to — and offer a deal to — Jorge Villa, the member of the Hand of Fate who had been given the harshest sentence. During the meal, they had decided on a plan that seemed to have the best chance of success. If the judge agreed to allow them to offer the deal that they had in mind, Sam and Jamie felt that they could get enough information on Clark to gain 'probable cause' for a search warrant of Clark's business facilities and his business records.

They felt fortunate that they got a judge who was receptive to granting the type of request for which Sam and Jamie had been hoping.

'Permission to proceed,' Judge Rollo said after hearing their arguments, 'provided the offer is limited to twenty-four hours, and the parameters adhere strictly to the guidelines you have stated. A visiting time will be arranged with the warden of the county men's prison, and you will be so informed. The twenty-four hours will begin five minutes later. Please be on time.'

Sam and Jamie had arrived early at the prison gate for their appointment with Jorge Villa. The guard had checked their

IDs and checked them off on the appointment list. Before he opened the gate, he handed them a sealed envelope.

'This is a written statement, signed by Judge Rollo, and a certified copy of the agreement to be offered to the prisoner. If accepted, return the original, countersigned by him and his attorney and leave the copy with them.

'Both copies will receive a date/time stamp, and you may begin your questions. The counsel for the prisoner may advise the refusal to answer any questions, so be precise in your wording.'

'Thank you,' Sam replied as he drove through the gate.

The visitor's room was sparsely furnished with a plain table and four chairs. A video recorder was set up near the ceiling opposite the entrance and had a view of the conference table and the door. The door locked behind them after they entered the room and sat down.

Before Sam sat down, he pulled out two cassette audio recorders from his briefcase. He also produced two microphones and plugged them into the recorders.

'These are special tamper-proof record-ings that cannot be copied,' he explained. 'The need for such precautions will be evident when you have read the proposed agreement in this envelope.'

Jamie opened the envelope and handed the two copies to the lawyer after glancing over both of them. 'Counselor,' she began, 'this document, and its certified copy, is a proposed agreement for early release for information about Stephen Clark, a.k.a. Clark Stephanos, that will aid us in our present investigations.'

Sam reached over and turned on the recorders and proceeded to give the time, date, and names of all of those present, along with the purpose of the recordings.

'Counselor,' Sam began, 'do you wish a few moments to review the agreement and to confer with your client?'

'Would five minutes be agreeable?' the lawyer asked.

'That is fine, Counselor,' Jamie answered after silently conferring with Sam. 'Would either of you like for us to bring you coffee or a Danish?'

'Nothing for me, thanks. Jorge, *una tasa de Café?*'

'*Si,*' Jorge answered. '*Gracias.*'

Sam and Jamie got up from their chairs. As Sam turned off the recorders, he signaled the guards to let them out. 'We'll be back in five minutes,' he told them.

As soon as the door closed, the attorney spoke to his client. 'This agreement is very specific in its terms, Jorge.' His face was a mask of seriousness. 'Essentially, they are allowed to ask any questions they wish about this person. I would cautiously recommend taking the deal. It means reducing the rest of your sentence by almost three months. The decision is still yours, though.'

'Stephen was one deadly *hombre,*' Jorge replied after a few moments. 'When we were in the same posse, he would slice you up good if he even thought you'd dissed him. They have to guarantee that he won't be able to get back at me! That Holmes *hombre,* he's the one who brought us down, even though Stephen was the only one not tried as an adult. If he says he can stop Stephen, him I will believe. I won't walk outta here until I ain't steppin' inta a death sentence!'

There was a knock at the door and Sam and Jamie walked in with three cups of coffee, plus packets of sweetener and non-dairy creamer.

Mr. Sandoval, the attorney, pointed to the recorders as Sam placed the coffees on the table and he and Jamie sat down.

'My client wishes to have certain concerns for his future safety addressed,' Sandoval said after the machines were restarted. 'After that, he will give you his answer. Are you willing to listen to his concerns?'

'We are willing to hear him out,' Sam replied. 'However, I cannot promise any absolutes. I will give my word of honor that Stephen will not learn of this deal from me.'

'And how 'bout yer partner, *Señor* Holmes?' Jorge responded. 'Is her word of honor also given?'

'It is, Mr. Villa,' Jamie told him. 'Two of our ancestors worked together and trusted their lives to one another, as though they were brothers. The honor of one is the honor of the other.'

'And your words of honor include doing your best to keep Stephen and any of his associates from exacting retribution upon my client?' Sandoval wished to know.

'Mr. Sandoval,' Jamie looked him straight in the eye, 'Clark and his associates have already made three attempts on the lives of members of my family as well as repeated attempts to do away with my partner. That makes it very personal that we ensure he and his friends are no longer in a position to come after anybody. Ever!'

'Take the deal,' Jorge told his attorney. ' 'Personal', I understand and trust.'

The next three hours were spent in gaining insight into the mind and motivations of Stephen Clark and his choice of associates.

When they were packing up to go, Sam gave one of the tapes to Sandoval and had him and Jorge sign both copies of the agreement. Then he had both signatures witnessed and notarized. Sandoval was then given a copy of the agreement.

'My client is to be released in three months?' Sandoval inquired.

'As agreed,' Jamie responded. 'We do not wish to give the appearance that his early release had anything to do with our visit today.'

'We look forward to never seeing you again,' Jorge told them. '*Buena suarte.*'

⋆　⋆　⋆

Sam and Jamie decided to stop at a Starbuck's and use the WiFi to correlate all of their new data on Stephen Clark's early activities and associates. They found out that three of his former associates (all of whom had served their full terms and therefore had no restrictions placed on their choices of compatriots) met at least twice a month at the Victorian Reading Room. Sometimes they would have lunch, other times they'd talk business or just socialize. They almost always used the same private corner. This provided not only a secure meeting place, but the club provided a reason for their getting together at unscheduled, as well as scheduled, times.

'The Diogenes Club of Mycroft Holmes' day had strict rules for membership and activities within the club's building,' Jamie observed. 'Does the Victorian Reading Room have any such restriction?'

'They do have a rule that women are not allowed in the 'Gentlemen Only' section; and, of course, they adhere to California law forbidding the use of tobacco products inside public buildings,' was Sam's response. 'We'll be using the public section anyway, so we shouldn't have any problems with management.'

When they arrived at the club, Sam and Jamie were greeted at the door by a man dressed in the uniform of a late-nineteenth-century butler. A generous tip got them a table in the public area with a good view of the other patrons. A waiter, also dressed in the Victorian style, took their drink orders and left them to themselves.

Two men at the nearby bar were

pretending not to notice the two detectives. They were both impeccably, if casually and conservatively, dressed in dark-colored blazers, turtleneck dressy-casual shirts, blue-black slacks with sharp creases, and shoes with a high-gloss shine.

'Those two gentlemen at the bar seem very interested in us,' Sam observed. 'I wonder what makes us so fascinating?'

'Why don't I invite them over to join us?' Jamie volunteered. 'Maybe they'd like our company.'

Jamie walked past the two men who had been watching her and Sam. As she approached their bar stools, she 'accidentally' tripped and fell against the men, causing them to spill their drinks.

'Oh,' she cried out as she clumsily righted herself, 'I'm so sorry! My heel must have snagged the carpeting. Please, join me and my friend at our table and allow us to replace your beverages.'

At first, the two men demurred, but they eventually allowed themselves to be persuaded. After ordering fresh drinks, Jamie led them to her table.

'My name is Jamie,' she said as they

approached Sam at their table. 'And this is my friend, Sam. Sam, these gentlemen's drinks are on us. I tripped on the carpeting and I caused them to spill their drinks when I fell against them.'

Sam stood up and extended his hand to each of them. The first man smiled as he shook Sam's hand in a firm, but friendless, grip.

'They call me Apollos,' he introduced himself, 'and my partner is known as Zeus. We're visiting people we know through our import-export business. Your lady friend's offer to replace our spilled drinks was most gracious and unexpected of her. Many Americans are such boors about manners.'

'My grandparents were from the Old World,' Jamie replied. 'I guess their values and ideas sorta rubbed off on me.'

Zeus' gaze fixed on Sam and Jamie in an icy stare as he said, 'Even the Old World has forgotten how to be gracious nowadays. Too many think only of themselves and not of others.'

Under the pretense of camaraderie between new friends, Sam and Jamie endeavored to learn what they could about the two men's backgrounds. Apollos claimed to be a software developer, and Zeus said he looked for new markets for his partner's products. Each offered the opinion that his field was rife with spies, thieves, and various other unscrupulous backstabbers.

'New developments in software are happening so fast,' Apollos commented, with a frown of frustration on his face, 'that it is hard to keep up with all of the changes. Programs and files used to be no more than a few thousand kilobytes, and took up to a full minute to load. Now, with new hardware they're running into many gigabytes, but not taking much longer to load than the old software.'

Jamie and Sam claimed to be vacationing members of a highly successful multi-level marketing company that provided a large number of products and services.

After twenty minutes or so, Apollos and Zeus excused themselves and left the club.

'An interesting pair,' Jamie remarked as

their impromptu guests made their exit. 'Did you notice how their eyes never settled on any object or person for more than a second or two?'

'Yes,' Sam answered quickly. 'I also noted that when they spoke of their backgrounds, that their body language didn't quite agree with their words.'

'Well, we figured that they weren't exactly what they seemed.' Jamie pursed her lips in recollection of the recent events. 'It did seem to me that their actions were a little off. More like they were seeking information rather than trying to hide anything.'

'Like, maybe, they are investigating the same group that we are?' Sam wondered. 'Just what have we gotten involved in?'

'The more we look into this, the more complicated it becomes!' Jamie heaved a frustrated sigh.

Sam's phone vibrated as a text message was received. He read the message, signaled the waiter for their bill, and then turned the phone where Jamie could read it.

Wireless electrodes found in debris

from fire, it read. *Fire investigators suspect arson.*

'The department techs who are reverse-engineering the super-Taser believe that it puts out twice the number of volts with three times the amps that are used in the electric chair,' Sam reported. 'That's why it's always been deadly once it made contact.'

'But how does it build that kind of charge?' wondered Jamie. 'There was no power pack found at the parking garage. And it couldn't hold a charge very long.'

'That's what the techs haven't been able to figure out yet,' a bewildered Sam replied. 'This was designed for the certain kill. The jolt not only paralyzes any organ it comes into contact with, but the more delicate ones will explode, causing an internal bleed-out.'

'You read Doctor Connor's report?'

'You were out of the squad room,' Sam informed her, 'so it was given to me. I looked it over before you got back.'

'I didn't know you were a medico,' Jamie said perturbedly.

'I took the advanced course in

emergency medicine at the academy,' he explained without emotion. 'I figured it would come in handy in a combat situation.'

'I got stuck with a modern Renaissance Man!' Jamie threw up her hands in mock frustration.

'Captain Valdez's partner might have survived that ambush if he'd had someone along with that kind of training,' Sam said coldly. 'It was thought that he just had a broken leg. Turned out that the large artery had been completely severed and he died from the internal hemorrhage.'

'Did you know him well?' Jamie asked repentantly.

'He was my mother's youngest cousin. He was only in his second year on the force.'

'Let's find a WiFi hotspot and correlate what we know.' Jamie decided that a change of subject would be a good idea just now.

24

After another two hours in the Victorian Reading Room, Sam looked at Jamie.

'Well, we now know that Clark hasn't exactly been an angel since his release from Juvenile Detention.' Sam straightened his long legs. 'Several of the deaths of the business owners whose businesses he acquired appeared suspicious at first, but were cleared later as suicides or accidents. Other acquisitions were very nasty hostile takeovers. Only about one percent were legitimate buy-outs of owners wanting to retire.'

'This security company he bought,' Jamie observed, 'was being investigated for questionable ethics of a major portion of their management people. He bought it for a song, then replaced the managers with his own people. The reputation has been restored and the business is growing.'

'Yeah,' Sam groused. 'But look at the

types of his new customers. All are high-powered munitions and weapons manufacturers. Wanna bet they've all had inventory discrepancies at one time or another since making their contracts with Clark Security?

'If we dig deep enough, we'll probably find that the missing ordinances showed up on the black market soon after Clark took a business trip to the area in question.'

The circumstantial evidence against Clark just kept growing. The solid, provable evidence was harder to find. Clark had learned well the art of hiding his trail.

★   ★   ★

The puffy-faced prisoner was processed into the system and then into a holding cell.

'Wot in 'ell 'appened to ya?' the taller and heavier of the two prisoners asked when he saw the bumps all over the face and arms of the new prisoner.

'That crazy Yank has a buncha trained

killer bees. They attacked me!' the man declared. 'There ain't 'nuff dough in th' world woulda paid me to tangle wi' th' Watson clan iffen I'd a knowed 'bout them bees!'

'Looks like third time ain't th' charm, eh, guys?' the short, skinny prisoner commented.

'Hush!' the first man hissed. 'These jail cells are all bugged and plugged inta video recorders nowadays.'

'Don't make no difference,' skinny said. 'I missed th' kid and got caught. I'm either dead or in lock-up forever no matter wot else 'appens. The Man don't give second chances, and don't 'cept no excuses.'

'Then I ain't leavin' this 'ere cell!' Puffy-face said. 'He cawn't get ta me wi'out bein' on camera. Better here than wi' them bees!'

'Now that's where you're wrong, gentlemen,' said a voice out of the shadows. 'The Man says 'good-bye'.' Three sharp buzzes sounded and each of the prisoners collapsed to the floor. The man in the shadows didn't stay to check his victims. He knew that they wouldn't be talking anymore. He left as silently and as invisibly as he had arrived. Before he had arrived, he had made sure that the surveillance devices wouldn't record anything that had just happened. He was home free. Or so he believed.

The next routine patrol and check of the cells found the three prisoners on the floor, their dead eyes staring at eternity.

'Check the surveillance recordings,' the head of the prison ordered. Word came quickly that someone had tampered with the equipment.

'Nothing but static,' the equipment technician reported, 'for about fifteen minutes, sir.'

The warden pointed to a hidden drawer.

'Check in there, Jacob,' he ordered.

Jacob looked surprised as he opened up the drawer that he had never known to exist. It contained a complete back-up of the original system. The warden retrieved the audio/visual disk from the machine. He used his special cellphone to contact the Scotland Yard inspector in charge of the Watsons' protection detail.

'The suspects are dead,' he told the inspector who answered the call. 'And the recording was tampered with. I have the back-up recording locked away in my desk.'

'I'll be there straight away,' the inspector replied.

⋆ ⋆ ⋆

The prison doctor was just finishing his examination when the inspector arrived.

'Any indication as to what killed them?' the inspector queried as he looked the scene over. 'The warden said that the recordings were full of static.'

'The only mark on them are these scorches on their shirts,' the doctor said, pointing to the marks, 'and a reddening of the skin underneath.'

'The FBI fellow said something about marks like these,' the inspector observed. 'I'll get in touch with him while you set up the postmortems.'

The inspector called the contact number he had for the FBI agents.

'Agent Roberts,' a male voice said after the connection was made.

'Agent Roberts,' the inspector began, 'This is Inspector Johnson. We have a case here at the prison near the Watsons' place on the Southern coast. Red mark on the skin and no other obvious signs of violence.'

'Has an autopsy been performed yet?'

'The prison doctor is preparing one for each of the three victims as we speak,' Johnson replied. 'The males were all arrested in relation to the attacks on you, your partner, and the Watsons.'

Robert's voice became colorless as he replied. 'If the weapon used was what I believe it was, the doctor will find burst organs and blood vessels at those sites. If so, then either a duplicate of an extra-powerful super-Taser has been made, or the one that we believe to still be in the States, has been brought over here. I'm contacting Sergeant Holmes and Doctor Watson. I think we're going to need them. They know more than anyone except the army about this.'

'Any relation to the Holmes and Watson

team from over a hundred and thirty years ago?' Inspector Johnson asked. 'I always heard that they were fictitious.'

'I couldn't say for sure,' Roberts told him just before he disconnected, 'but Doctor Watson is the daughter of the Doctor Watson that you know down there. I'll leave for your location in about an hour.'

Caleb Roberts walked through the connecting door into Sarah Thorsdatter's room.

'The super-Taser may have been smuggled into this country,' he said as he walked over to the chair near the bed where his partner was sitting and recuperating from her wound. 'The three suspects were found dead in their cells, with marks suspiciously similar to the ones that are believed to be made by the super-Taser. I've made a call to California. Sam and Jamie hope to be on a plane to Heathrow as soon as they can tie up some loose ends on the case at their end. I'm headed down there to get more first-hand information.'

'Think that the docs'll let me go with

you?' Sarah stood up and headed to her bedroom to change. 'I promise to be a good girl and not rip out my stitches or anything.'

'The more eyes on this case,' Caleb grinned, 'the better, I say.'

A quick train ride later, the two FBI agents were sitting in Inspector Johnson's office.

'You were correct about the internal damage,' Johnson informed them. 'All three had extensive damage to heart, lungs, and the aortic artery. The doctor said that if their hearts hadn't stopped beating instantly, they would have bled out in seconds. Nasty weapon, that.'

'Fortunately, it has a very limited range,' Caleb told the inspector. 'The wireless electrodes are ejected by a compressed gas chamber, and the range of the power signal is only a few meters.'

25

Jamie looked over the notes that she and Sam had taken during their interview with Jorge Villa.

'This man who calls himself Greco Spartos,' Jamie mused out loud, 'sounds like one of the Black Knights. Didn't you say that one of them disappeared just before the arrests of the Hand of Fate?'

'Yes.' Sam took note of the man that Jamie had mentioned. 'Several members of the Black Hand had been implicated in the activities as accomplices. There was no conclusive proof that the two gangs were working together, but several members of both gangs were arrested.

'Villa said that Spartos was the peacemaker between the two gangs just before everyone got caught in your net. Several people thought that he had betrayed both sides.'

'But he disappeared almost two weeks before the bust went down, and I know that we had no informants from either gang. I had pieced together information based on overheard conversations and inferences that the deal was going down,' Sam recalled. 'It was pretty ambitious for either gang, but from what I knew of Clark, I believed that the rumors and innuendos were most likely true. I was proven right and, for all practical purposes, put the two gangs out of business.'

'Okay,' Jamie responded, 'how do we put Clark behind bars?'

'This looks to be his most vulnerable business,' Sam pointed at one that seemed to have many international links, 'and it fits right in with what I just heard from Agent Roberts.'

'Don't keep me in suspense.' Jamie playfully gave Sam the evil eye. 'What's going on?'

'Our three assassin suspects were all found dead in their cells.' Sam ignored Jamie's expression. 'The super-Taser may have been used to kill them. Lieutenant Colonel Rembrandt has talked to Lieutenant Baker and the commissioner. We leave for Heathrow as soon as we can, and then on to your parents' bee farm.'

'Actually, Dad told me that the property belongs to you,' Jamie told a startled Sam. 'The bee farm is where Sherlock Holmes retired after he broke up the Kaiser's spy ring just before the Great War. Your great-grandmother had inherited the property next door. That's where she and Holmes first met. The properties have been under a caretakership since your grandfather's and your father's day. The incomes from the properties have been held in trust for you and your heirs, according to your father's will.'

'I knew about the trust and the British property,' Sam told her. 'I never thought about it much. I had work that I liked doing and I felt that I was financially secure, so I just allowed things to go on as they always had. I thought of the place as a possible retirement project.'

'My parents were asked by the villagers if they wanted to lease the property when they moved to England. As descendants of the original Doctor Watson they were only asked to pay the legal minimum for the lease.'

26

Greco Spartos watched the farmhouse through his special field glasses. The five individuals he had under surveillance seemed to have a routine that varied little from day to day. Twice a week, the younger of the two men would leave on the earliest train to London and return on the midday run the next day.

The older man often played with the young boy, teaching him about bees and other animals connected with the two farms. Occasionally, the family would take visits to the village or have visitors from the village. These would often be to or from young families with children close to the boy's age. The children did what all young children did when they got together. At other times, the older couple would have visits from their friends in the village.

Today, he noted a change. Two strangers and the local inspector had come by after breakfast and hadn't left by the time that it got dark. Greco concluded that it would be likely that they would spend the night. The woman's right arm and shoulder appeared stiff, and the male stranger kept checking the area until they went inside the house.

He decided that these strangers were the law enforcers from America. This would not change the timing of his plans he decided. He would do it tonight.

As darkness fell, Greco moved stealthily, taking care not to approach the beehives too closely. As he neared the wall of the house without windows, he opened a large container of clear liquid. The liquid was a special odorless accelerant. He began to saturate the wall and ground with it. He was certain that his plan would work.

Just as he was about to set fire to the accelerant, he heard a loud snap and felt a severe pain in his left ankle. The interior lights came on as he heard a voice come out of the darkness of the yard.

'Stay absolutely still,' the voice commanded. 'If you move, you'll just lose your foot if you're lucky. Now, put out the match, and place your hands on top of your head with your fingers interlaced. *Now!*'

Greco did as he was told, the pain in his leg leaving him in no mood to argue. He just wanted the pain to stop!

Joe quickly placed Caleb's zip cuffs on Greco's wrists and secured his hands behind his back.

'My friend is a retired medical man,' Greco was informed as he was helped to his feet and into the house. 'He'll see to your ankle. Now, tell me what you were doing sneaking around. It's not like you were lost or anything.'

'I don't have to tell you anything!' Greco spat out his words between gasps of pain. 'You ain't no cop!'

'And I don't have to let you have medical attention, either,' Joe remarked without emotion, 'since you were trespassing with harmful intent on private property in the middle of the night. There have been some very dangerous animals loose around here recently. You stepped on one of the traps. We are not as accommodating to criminals here as they are in the US.'

After Jonathan treated Greco's leg, the village constable formally arrested the man and took him to the local jail. It didn't take long for Greco to admit that he had intended to burn the house down with all occupants inside, even though he would not give the name of the person who had paid him to do so. During the search of the prisoner's personal belongings, an unusual device was found.

'What do you think o' this?' the officer asked Joe and Jonathan. 'Looks like some kinda stun gun.'

'Could be the super-Taser my daughter and her partner told James about,' Jonathan told them. 'Very dangerous and stealthy.'

'They're certain to be awake, John,' Joe said thoughtfully as he looked at his watch and stroked his chin. 'Maybe you should call them. And tell them that the man we have in custody is the same one as on the back-up video.'

The call to California was answered on the second ring.

'Hi, Dad,' Jamie answered cheerfully, but with a little concern when she saw the caller ID. 'Is everyone OK? It's fairly late in London, isn't it?

'Just about two in the morning here,' her father informed her. 'We may have the other super-Taser and the man who used it on those prisoners. He stepped on one of the animal traps when he attempted arson on the house. Everyone is fine and the house is unharmed.'

'We were checking out a man calling himself Greco Spartos,' Sam said over the phone's speaker function. 'He seems to have disappeared.'

'The man that is in custody has identification under that name,' Jonathan told his daughter's partner. 'His passport is from the States. Do you think that he could be the same one that you're looking for?'

'He could very well be, sir,' was Sam's response. 'We think this person could be our best lead on Clark's activities and connections.'

As soon as they disconnected from Jamie's dad, she and Sam made arrangements with their superiors for a plane trip to England.

'A US marshal will be traveling with you,' Captain Reynolds, who had been sitting in on their plans, told them. 'He, or she, will have the necessary papers for extradition if we should need him back here for any reason. Our friends on the other side of the Atlantic are fairly accommodating. Let's hope that this Greco Spartos is just as helpful.'

Captain Reynolds told Sam and Jamie that their tickets would be available at the British Airways ticket counter in two days.

'It seems as though everyone is after this super-Taser thief,' the captain commented as they got up to exit the office. 'The commissioner has been notified that two Interpol agents are in the country seeking information.'

'Perhaps we met them at the Victorian Reading Room,' Sam told him. 'We were checking a theory at the club when we noticed two foreigners surreptitiously watching us from the bar in the public area.'

'They gave their names as Apollos and Zeus,' Jamie added. 'They were here on business. A software developer and his marketing partner.'

'Could have been them,' Captain Reynolds said. 'Remember that the military and the FBI are involved in this, too. The way this is shaping up, I wouldn't be surprised if half the country's intelligence and law enforcement entities aren't already involved in this.'

'And, of course,' Sam noted, 'everyone is working at cross-purposes, playing their cards close to their vests.'

'Just watch your backs,' was the captain's last comment as they all left the building.

27

After Jamie checked the British Airways site online, and verified their flight schedule out of Ontario International, she called her parents and told them when her flight was expected to arrive.

'Sam has never been to his ancestors' home,' she told her father. 'He was thinking of possibly retiring there in the distant future, but hadn't really made up his mind. He says he's looking forward to meeting you and seeing little Jimmy again. The two of them really hit it off when we were in Vegas.'

They chatted a little longer and then, before Jonathan said goodbye, he told her, 'We'll meet you at the restaurant where your brother and his family spent their first night in England.'

★ ★ ★

Two days later, Sam and Jamie were at the British Airways counter picking up their tickets and checking in their luggage. As they were walking to the waiting lounge, a tall, dark man with a well-proportioned physique greeted them. From the inside pocket of his well-fitted blazer, he pulled out a wallet with a badge and credentials.

'Newton Fox, US Marshal's office,' he introduced himself. 'I understand that we will be fellow passengers on this flight.'

'Detective Sergeant Holmes.' Sam took the other man's offered hand. 'And this is Doctor Watson. We're both from the London, CA police department. We were told that you would be carrying papers for the extradition of Greco Spartos.'

'That's correct, Sergeant Holmes,' Marshal Fox replied. 'I understand that your family will be meeting us, Doctor Watson?'

'That's true,' Jamie answered. 'My father retired to an English bee farm that Sam's great-grandfather owned early in the twentieth century.'

'Ah, yes.' Marshal Fox smiled pleasantly. 'I grew up on the stories that were written by Conan Doyle. I never thought I'd meet any of Holmes' or Watson's relatives.'

The three of them compared notes on Greco Spartos and how recent events related to the, until now, secret super-Taser weapon.

'Deadlier than a knife,' Fox observed, 'and nearly as quiet. An assassin's dream weapon. Any idea how it was gotten away from the military?'

'According to second-hand information,' Jamie explained, 'a surprise inventory check was made, and the prototypes were discovered missing. Soon after that, and in quick succession, three unexplained deaths occurred.'

Jamie and Sam both told of the events that had led up to the present situation until their flight was called for passengers to board.

'Will we be allowed to keep our weapons?' Sam asked the marshal after they had strapped themselves into their seats. 'I'm not familiar with the rules for weapons over there.'

'A lot will depend on the relationship

of our purpose for entering their country, and our specific instructions from our government,' Fox explained. 'The weapons may have to be kept in their lockboxes and stored in Scotland Yard's security locker until we leave, or we may be given special carry permits. We won't know until we go through customs.'

Since it would be a long flight, Jamie and Sam went over their notes with Marshal Fox, bringing him up to speed on their investigation and what they theorized about the Golden BBs and the John Brown Society.

'The Department of Justice and Homeland Security feel as you do that the John Brown Society are being used as patsies for the BBs' agenda,' he informed them. 'The government has been trying for a long time to get enough information on the leadership of the BBs to bring down the organization and as many of their associates as they can. Interpol and EU people have tried, without success, to infiltrate various cells of the group.'

'The man we believe to head the BBs is an old acquaintance of mine,' Sam told

Fox. 'When I was with the police explorers, I helped to get enough evidence against him, his teenage gang, and their former rivals to put most of them away as adults. That was about ten years ago. Clark's lawyer was able to get him tried as a minor instead of an adult like the rest of his associates. Now, as an adult, he appears to be rehabilitated into a prosperous, and well-respected, pillar of society. His wealth and position make it hard to accuse him of any malfeasance.'

'The rich can afford to insulate themselves with lawyers,' Jamie opined, 'whether they are law-abiding or not, and unfortunately, many of them are very good at obeying the letter, but not the spirit of the law. But then, human nature seems to lean toward self-indulgence rather than altruism.'

After their layover in New York, the three police officers decided to nap for the rest of the trip so as to help overcome the jet lag.

When the plane landed, Sam, Jamie, and Newton gathered up their luggage and got a cab to the hotel and restaurant where they were to meet Jamie's family.

Little Jimmy was excited to see his aunt and her friend. He was also quick to make a new friend of the US Marshal.

'I have lots of policeman friends now,' the excited boy told him. 'I've got a lot of new friends to play with, too, from where Grandma and Grandpa live. They all came to my birthday party! I also saw Bossy become a mama cow! I've had lots of fun and learned so many new things!'

Jamie looked toward the entrance. A tall, well-dressed woman who appeared to be in her thirties, was greeted by the host and led to an empty table.

'Sam,' she whispered to him as she nudged his arm to get his attention. 'Do you see that woman just being seated?'

'You mean,' Sam whispered back, 'the blond in the blue pantsuit and fancy sandals? What about her?'

'She's cleaned herself up, changed her hairstyle and its color, and appears sane now, but I'm positive that's the same woman that the airport security had to escort out of the building when we were in Vegas with the FBI decoys.'

'The one who was preaching doom for all the sinners invading the realm of the natural creatures of the air?'

'Yes,' Jamie assured him. 'I don't like it that she's here in England right now.'

'Perhaps,' Jonathan spoke up, 'the local BSI5 can get us some answers.'

'BSI5?' Marshal Fox was puzzled. 'Who, or what, are they? Some secret British agency?'

'No.' Jonathan grinned. 'Just the current generation of street kids the Yard uses to keep up with the local scuttlebutt. They're named after Sherlock Holmes' original Baker Street Irregulars. The kids earn some honest cash, and the law gets useful street intelligence. The intelligence agencies were able to foil and capture several spies from the Central and Axis powers during both World Wars with their help. Brave kids as well as smart.'

★ ★ ★

As the group left the restaurant, Jonathan stopped by a girl with a shoeshine box.

'I'll give you a full crown for a shine,

and information on the best places to entertain my guests from the States.' He smiled at the teenage girl, and gently pulled at his ear as he sat down on a bench.

'What do yer friends like?' she asked as she put her folding stool down in front of him and began her work. 'I see ya got a little one wit' ya. Want him entertained, but keep th' grown-ups 'appy, too, Guv?'

'Something like that,' Jonathan spoke softly. 'Somewhere we can be free of child thieves and the like as well. A blond woman in a blue suit has been following us all day.'

'Right,' the girl said as she finished shinning Jonathan's shoes. ''Ad to tell th' coppers 'bout such a character th' other week who was followin' a kid from the school house. Littles like 'im don't know the signs very well yet. It's up to us olders to watch over 'em while they learn. Do I turn 'er in?'

'No,' Jonathan told her after a moment's thought. 'Learn as much as you can about her and leave the information in the old number-five bolthole. Someone will check there in a day or two.'

'Done, sir.' The girl quietly accepted the extra half crown tip Jonathan gave her. 'The little 'un wit' ya might like the afternoon show at the petting zoo. Lotsa fun facts that th' adults'll like too.'

'So that was one of the BSI5?' Fox inquired as they left the plaza. 'How do you tell them from the rest of the kids running the street?'

'Unless you've been introduced by someone they already know and trust, you can't tell them from the other tuffs on the street. Most of them fell through the cracks in the system until the Yard or the local constabulary recruited them. All children are required to spend a certain number of hours in school learning a trade and the basics of an education. A lot of teenagers get set up as shoeshines, bicycle repair people, or in small engine repair. Jasmine likes to travel the city and meet people.

'My friend, Joe, saved her from a child predator when she was about nine years old. He taught her how to recognize when she was being followed, and to recognize when others were in danger. She's also one of only five people that I've taught the art of baritsu.'

28

Jimmy found the petting zoo performance to be entertaining. The baby elephant played a game that her trainer had taught her, and received lots of applause from the audience and a special treat from her trainer as well as lots of loving praise and affectionate pats and strokes.

Everyone was amazed at the tricks performed by the trained seals, dolphins, and dogs.

'It looks like someone is getting tired.' Alicia started to pick up her sleepy-eyed son just as a blond woman dressed in blue dashed up, knocked Alicia down, and grabbed Jimmy.

'Anyone comes near me, and I hurt the boy!' She held the struggling, and no longer sleepy, child.

'Jimmy,' James told him, 'bad person! Fight *now*. Fight *hard*!'

The seemingly easily-controlled child grabbed the woman's nearest hand and bent the fingers back as hard as he could, stomped on her toes, and kicked her shins. When the woman slapped Jimmy's face, he bit down on the hand he had grabbed as hard as he could instead of submitting or crying.

The other adults had now surrounded the woman, and held her until one of the police officers arrived to determine what the commotion was about.

'Bad woman tried to steal Jimmy!' the boy yelled as soon as he saw the uniformed officer. 'Papa say fight! Jimmy fight just like Papa taught!'

Tears were running down Jimmy's cheeks, and his left cheek was beginning to turn red and starting to swell as he asked, 'Did Jimmy do good, Papa? Did Jimmy fight hard?'

James picked up his crying son and gave him the biggest hug he could, grateful that the slap had been his only injury.

'Yes, Jimmy,' James praised his son and wept on his shoulder. 'You did *very* good — you fought as hard as a five-year-old, and you've only just turned three!'

★ ★ ★

All of the Watson entourage had decided to take rooms at the local bed and breakfast after making statements about the attempted kidnapping. A grubby-looking vagrant followed them, and then melted into the darkness.

'Those two families are just too damned lucky,' he muttered to himself. 'First Greco gets caught in an animal trap, and then a three-year-old fights off a grown woman long enough for her to get caught. Well, Shirley, you got what you deserved if you couldn't handle a little kid.'

Stephen Clark, a.k.a. Clark Stephanos, turned hate-filled eyes back toward the cottage where his enemies were staying. As he stood hidden in the dark, a bicycle patrolman rode by and Clark left as silently as he had come.

29

Everyone was having a hard time getting to sleep after the attempted kidnapping. Jimmy said that when he closed his eyes, he could see the 'bad woman' trying to take him away. All of the adult Watsons were on a heightened state of alert after the ordeal. Sam, Jamie, and Newton talked late into the night, attempting to fit the woman into the puzzle the super-Taser case had become.

'All of these attacks on you, Jamie, and her family have all seemed to be well-planned,' Newton commented after hearing a summary of the last few weeks. 'And I've never heard of this 'Hugo Langsman' you say informed you about the plot against Professor Watson and his family. Did he tell you the name of the group he is supposed to represent?'

'No,' Jamie confessed as she recalled the conversation with Langsman. 'He claimed to belong to a completely dark branch of criminal investigators. He behaved very cloak-and-daggerish.'

'And he was the one who told us about the John Brown Society,' added Sam. 'We knew almost nothing about them until he told us. I, for one, had never heard of John Brown or his attack on Harper's Ferry.'

'You say that you knew Clark Stephanos when you were a teenager, Sam,' Marshal Fox inquired. 'What kind of person was he back then?'

'An intelligent young man who had graduated two years early,' Sam replied. 'He was alleged to have been the warlord and strategic planner for the Hand of Fate.'

Sam told Fox all about his experiences with the Police Explorers and his part in thwarting the plans of the Black Knights and the Hand of Fate to form a crime cartel in the Jurupa Valley. He told how Stephen Clark's lawyer had convinced the judge to try him as a minor, and then to agree to let his sentence end upon his reaching the age of majority. None of the other lawyers were successful in their attempts to do the same. All of the others were tried, convicted, and sentenced as adults.

The information provided by Jorge Villa had placed Clark's activities after being released as well planned hostile takeovers and forced buyouts of the businesses he and his cohorts had targeted earlier. The earlier strong-arm and threat tactics had been refined, and not one of the former owners had been able to file a successful complaint against the new proprietors.

'Sounds like Clark learned a lot during his time in juvie,' Newton remarked after hearing Sam's story. 'Mr. Villa sounds like he could have made a good undercover agent if he'd been inclined to work on the legal side of the street.'

'He was probably the second smartest man in either of the two gangs,' Sam agreed. 'Jorge thinks that Clark set him up to take the hardest fall when their scheme failed. He claims that Clark may have attempted to have him eliminated at least three times during his imprisonment.'

'He and Clark both belong to the 'never forgive, never forget' philosophy,' Jamie spoke up. 'That's why we were so exact when we made our promises when making our deal. We made sure that he and his lawyer had full access to written and audio copies of our conversations. We also arranged that he was to be placed in a super-max security cell until his early release three months after Clark's arrest and conviction.'

'Sounds like everyone's got their sixes covered.' The marshal's face was grim.

⋆ ⋆ ⋆

When Marshal Fox presented his credentials and papers requesting extradition, the three law officers from the US were taken to an interview room and allowed to meet with the man known as Greco Spartos.

'Hello, Bubba,' Sam said as soon as he saw the man who was brought into the room. 'Imagine meeting you here after all of this time. Jamie, Newton, meet Bubba O'Reilly, the only man to avoid arrest more than a decade ago.'

'Samuel Holmes,' Bubba sneered, 'the man who claimed he wasn't qualified to teach the fighting technique he obviously knew so well. I hear that you made sergeant of detectives and are currently on the fast track to make lieutenant.'

'And I can still bring down your old buddy Stephen Clark — or, as he's now known, Clark Stephanos. Funny, neither of you had Greek backgrounds when I pulled the plug on your dreams of a criminal empire back then.'

'The triple Cs were ripe for a takeover by the right people,' Bubba snapped back. 'The Greek connection seemed to be the quickest and easiest way to do it.'

'Marshal,' Sam looked at the lawman, 'this man is still wanted as a fugitive in the United States, and can now be considered to have fled the country to avoid arrest and prosecution. I think you have plenty of reason to take him into custody and transport him back to the States.'

★ ★ ★

While the conference in the interview room was being held, the FBI and several Riverside County specialist teams were quietly surrounding a large farmhouse near the eastern county line. Inside were believed to be several high-ranking members of the John Brown Society.

At the given prearranged signal, tear gas grenades and flash-bangs were lofted through several windows. The stunned and disabled occupants were taken into custody, read their rights, and soon delivered to local places of incarceration, there to wait on being officially informed of the charges being placed against them after each individual was identified.

'That went a lot more smoothly than we anticipated,' SAC Jones told Captain Reynolds. 'I thought for sure these people would give us more of a hard time.'

'Yes,' Captain Reynolds responded, grateful that none of his people had taken fire or serious injury. 'If the interrogations work out the same way, we could wrap this up very quickly. Maybe they'll bring down the Golden BBs with them.'

'We live in hope, Captain,' Jones

agreed. 'FYI, Zeus and Apollos turned out to be undercover agents from the European Union division of Interpol. It seems that the 'Biblical Brothers' and a relative who goes by the name of 'Lemech' have been very bad boys over in Greece. Interpol has now checked 'Abel' off of their list of criminals wanted for international crimes and possible weapons trafficking. They'll be very glad to get the rest.'

The interrogations of the captured members of the John Brown Society did, indeed, yield better than expected results, but not nearly as good as hoped. Those captured were not as well informed as they had pretended to be. However, the leads that led to the arrests of low level members of the Golden BBs had added to the increasing knowledge of the group's activities, and in some cases, to new suspects to watch.

30

The three men who met regularly with Clark Stephanos at the Victorian Reading Room, and Clark himself, had all taken recent business trips to various European, Near Eastern, and Middle Eastern countries.

Two of the men had itineraries that would have them arriving soon after Clark. All three would be in London at the same time that Sam, Jamie, and Marshal Fox were scheduled to meet Jamie's family.

The morning after the meeting with 'Greco', Sam was on the phone to the other London.

'From what we now suspect, and believe,' Lieutenant Baker informed him, 'Clark, and two men known as 'Deimos' and 'Phobos', are all expected to arrive in England at any time, if they're not there already. I want all of you to grow eyes in the backs of your heads. The two Interpol agents you and Jamie ran into in the Victorian Reading Room have been found dead in their rooms under suspicious circumstances. You, Jamie, and her family members are the most likely targets next on the list.'

'Have any other members of the BBs been captured?' Jamie asked over the speaker-phone.

'From what Scotland Yard has told us,' Lieutenant Baker answered, 'Lemech may have been one of those three killed in the prison.'

'Greco Spartos, the suspected killer,' Sam reported, 'has turned out to be Bubba O'Reilly, a fugitive from the days of the Black Knights and the Hand of Fate. He was the only one to escape when I was with the Police Explorers. We now have 'fleeing to avoid arrest' to add to the extradition papers.'

'How's Jamie's nephew?' Lieutenant Baker changed the thrust of his call. 'I saw on Skype and CNN news about a brave little boy who fought off an alleged kidnapper until adult family members could capture her. I'm assuming that was young Master Watson?'

'A bit traumatized and lot scared,' Jamie told him. 'We're all proud of the way he held back his fear and did what my brother had taught him to do from the time he turned two. Until this happened, I think Jimmy thought it was just a game that he only played with his father. When the woman slapped him, I think Jimmy realized that it wasn't a game to the 'bad person'. No one had ever slapped him in the face before. Thank God, the shock made him mad instead of making him freeze.'

31

Two days later, the American Peace Officers got to interrogate the woman and Greco, a.k.a. Bubba, one after the other.

'And what shall I call you?' the US Marshal asked. 'I don't think 'Hey You' or 'Lady' is very flattering.'

'Why not just call me after that little girl actress from the thirties?' She gave them a nasty smirk. 'You know, Shirley Temple. I always loved to watch her sing and dance.'

'I don't think that the late Mrs. Black would approve,' Fox told her. 'I think I'll just refer to you as 'Shirley Doe'.'

'Whatever.'

'What were you doing in the Las Vegas Airport when Security escorted you out of the building?' Jamie prompted. 'I heard your little speech as they removed you from the lobby.'

'What I was paid to do.' Shirley took out a cigarette and put it in her mouth.

'Find out where you parked, and make sure you didn't come back and interrupt anything.'

'No smoking allowed in the interrogation rooms, miss,' the female guard told her authoritatively. 'The smoke messes up the electronics'

'Well, la-di-da!' Shirley threw her cigarette on the floor and crushed it under her shoe.

'And did the same people pay you to kidnap my partner's nephew?' Sam scowled, not very sympathetic given the woman's attitude.

'Yeah,' she sneered back at him. 'Who'd a thought that a three-year-old could be so nasty a fighter? He almost broke my fingers, and his teeth nearly drew blood. I hope he's had his shots!'

'Since the said three-year-old was only defending himself against your felonious actions,' Fox calmly told her, 'and you, as an adult, are several times larger and stronger than he, I see no reason for you to complain.

'Now why don't you tell us about your employer? What did he, or she, look or sound like? How were you contacted and how were you paid?'

'How 'bout you take your questions and stuff 'em where the sun don't shine, 'Marshal Dillon'?' Shirley, in a most unladylike manner, spat on the floor. ''The Man' will take care of me.'

'Just like he had Greco take care of the three men unfortunate enough to get caught, too?' Jamie chided, hoping for a reaction. 'They were super-Tasered right in their cells.'

Shirley's face turned pale, but she remained silent. Sam and Jamie looked at her, and then at each other.

'We all know that Clark isn't in the habit of leaving the trash uncollected,' Sam sighed as he got up from his chair. 'It's been a real non-pleasure to have met you, Shirley. I don't think we'll get another chance to talk. Clark now is either in the UK, or will be arriving shortly. Since Greco has been captured, too, he'll probably do you himself. I know for a fact that he doesn't mind getting his hands bloody.' Sam turned to the others. 'I think we've done all we can here.'

The Americans rose from their chairs to leave. As they prepared to walk out of the door, the female guard helped the prisoner to her feet, preparatory to escorting her back to her cell.

'Wait!' Shirley called out, a look of fear and panic now on her face. 'Don't let him come after me. Please! Clark won't be kind enough to just use the super-Taser on me. He'll want me to bleed out slowly and painfully.'

'We promise to do what we can, but we're only human,' Fox told her honestly. 'Tell us all that you know about him and his organization and we'll do our best to get him before he gets you.'

'Put that promise in writing. I'll sign it, and any waivers of legal representation, in exchange for any protection you can provide. I'll tell you everything I know about dear Lover Boy.'

Everyone sat back down. The audio recording of Shirley's plea and Marshal Fox's agreement was taken and transcribed while they waited in silence. After a minute or two, multiple copies of the transcribed agreement were brought back for the appropriate signatures.

After all of the copies were signed by all parties and witnessed, the audio and visual recorders were checked to make sure that they were operating properly and set to recording mode. All of the proper opening statements and questions were made according to legal procedures.

Shirley began by giving her true name and the fact that she had been living with the man she knew as Clark Stephanos for three years. She continued by giving the names of many of Clark's confederates and the dates of many of his business activities, legal and illegal. A goodly number of her facts had been verified by many of the captured members of the John Brown Society.

'Clark always treated me as just another blond bimbo,' Shirley complained. 'He never gave any thought as to what I might have in my head about his plans or his organization.

'He believes that he's so smart, but I know how he and his gang was brought down by that Police Explorer when he was in his teens.'

'If anyone can stop Clark,' Jamie told her, 'it's Samuel Holmes. He's the one who put Clark's plans through the shredder year's ago.'

'I certainly hope you know where he is, 'cause you're gonna need him.'

'He's right here in front of you,' Sam responded. 'I hope to make history repeat itself, and soon.'

★ ★ ★

Clark was plotting how he would make Greco and Shirley pay for their failures. Perhaps he could get some rat poison and sneak it into their food. He didn't have much time before both of them would be on a plane back to the States, he knew. The extradition papers had all been signed and approved according to the reports from his spies from inside the prison. He was certain that Greco wouldn't tell anything he knew about Clark's 'business' endeavors, but there was no room for people who got caught in his plans. It was too bad, because Greco had been his best and most faithful lieutenant.

324

Now, Shirley was different. She'd been fun and willing to do anything he asked of her, both in and out of the bedroom. But he knew she was weak and could be easily turned against him. He would have to eliminate her quickly and painfully. He had no use for fawning sycophants. Besides, she was beginning to bore him. She would have had to be taken care of soon anyway. He would kill her tonight, or tomorrow night at the latest.

Feeling better now that he had made his decision, he went to the nearby pub for a pint and a game of darts.

★   ★   ★

As Sam, Jamie, and Marshal Fox were walking out of the prison, Sam was unsettled. His subconscious alarms were jangling his perceptions as if they had a physical reality.

'Have Shirley's and Greco's food tested for poison and foreign objects,' he asked the warden. 'Clark won't want either of them to be alive to give us any information that they know. If he finds out that Shirley has already been turned, what he does to her won't just be a slap on the wrist. And watch your employees. His spies are already here. That's how Greco could get to those three men without being caught on the main surveillance tapes.

'Your Doctor Who's nemesis, the Master, could not be more evil or ruthless. This man is as cold and unfeeling as a human being can be. Moriarty, Hitler, and Stalin were children compared to him.'

The warden lifted his eyebrows, but quickly gave the orders.

'The two American prisoners are to be double-guarded and no one and nothing, including food trays, are to enter their cells without being thoroughly searched and/or tested,' he told the assistant warden. 'All clearances and work histories are to be reviewed immediately. No one with less that five years seniority at *this* prison is to go within a hundred meters of these two until they're taken to the airport. I don't want any trustees or other prisoners even in the same cell block. Get it done. Get it done *last week!*'

The assistant warden hurried to implement his superior's orders. The American prisoners were placed in maximum security cells with a double compliment of guards with unimpeachable records on a 24/7 schedule.

When the food trays came, special equipment was used to test the different portions of the meal for poisons, ground glass, and other foreign items that could be harmful or cause a deadly reaction. The prisoners had also been questioned about food and drug allergies. Clark would have to work very hard if he wished to harm his subordinates.

'We have everything as secure as we can make it,' the warden told Sam and his group when everything was ready. 'Even when you were interviewing Greco Spartos the second time, he had extra security and he was searched afterward for anything that he could use to destroy himself. His new cell has been cleared of any harmful, or potentially deadly, items. Even a fly would have trouble getting in to either of them.'

'Don't relax your vigilance until we have them in the air and headed back home,' Newton advised. 'Two corpses won't help us any, and will just put us back to square one.'

* * *

Three figures in nighttime camouflage quietly approached the perimeter of the prison.

'The ceramic knife and the cyanide have got to be smuggled in past all of the extra precautions being used,' Clark whispered to the men with him. 'You're sure that the tunnel will get us where we need to be?'

'Our people inside have assured us that it will, and that it hasn't been discovered yet.'

Unbeknownst to the three intruders or their spies, an ultrasound of the cells and under the flooring had been done, and revealed the tunnel. A special watch had been set up to keep an eye and ear on the tunnels using motion and sound detectors.

When Clark and his men entered the tunnel around midnight, the silent alarms were set off and a squad of men entered the prison end of the tunnel with the intention of keeping the intruders out of the special cells.

As the two groups silently approached each other in the dark, Sam and Newton made their way to the outside tunnel mouth to head off any attempt to escape.

The warden's men were using low-light goggles to keep their presence from being given away by the use of lanterns or any other source of light in the dark.

Clark and his men had memorized the route that they needed to take. Both groups were able to move at almost a normal pace and were soon to meet each other.

Just before coming to a bend in the tunnel, Clark halted and signaled his men to do the same. He listened for a moment, and then started pushing his men back to the outside.

'I heard the sound of men coming toward us,' he whispered. 'The tunnel has been found and turned into a trap. We have to get out before they find us.'

Clark, Deimos, and Phobos drew out their knives, and their silenced and stealthy handguns, as they quickly and quietly made their way back outside.

As they reached the opening, a voice in the dark spoke as a bright searchlight was turned on them.

'You are ordered in the name of the Crown to lay down your arms and surrender,' Inspector Johnson's authoritative bass told them.

'Give up,' Sam added. 'The inspector, marshal, and I have you and your men surrounded. The Browns and the BBs have all been captured or are on the run.'

Marshal Fox also told them, ' 'Ares' was shot down in Lisbon when he refused to surrender to Interpol agents. The three of you are the last of the group's leadership.'

Deimos raised his weapon and began firing randomly at the voices. Phobos aimed at the search light, hoping to shoot it out before his enemies had him targeted.

He did put out the light, but not before being struck by several bullets himself.

Clark dove to the ground and took aim at the muzzle flashes as bullets whizzed overhead and kicked up dirt nearby. He saw Deimos stagger and fall, then heard Phobos scream as he was hit several times just before the big light went dark.

Crawling toward the cover of an outbuilding near the edge of the exercise yard, Clark heard Sam's voice just a few meters off to this right. Knowing that escape was unlikely, Clark decided that he would take his nemesis with him if he had to die this night. For die he *would* before he allowed himself to be captured.

'Clark!' Sam was telling him, 'Give yourself up. Your men are dead or disabled and you can't escape. We have at least fifteen men from Scotland Yard with us. Your spies are being rounded up by the warden's best, and most trusted, men. Shirley told us everything she knew about your group of upscale cutthroats, thieves, and bullies.'

Clark crept as silently as possible toward the sound of his enemy's voice. When he finally spied the silhouette of a human form, he pulled out his blade and worked his way behind the almost invisible form.

He leaped on the back of the person in front of him and realized that the person was not an armed man, but an unarmed woman.

Even better, he thought. He would do better than to kill the last Holmes. He would kill a Watson, and leave Holmes the rest of his life to regret her death because he had dared to cross paths again with Stephen Clark, a.k.a. Clark Stephanos.

★   ★   ★

Jamie heard the rustle of feet on the pathway behind her in time to deflect the knife blade from her back and into her shoulder.

Uttering a scream of pain, she twisted and kicked at her assailant as she was knocked to the ground.

'One less Watson in the world after tonight,' she heard a harsh male voice growl at her.

'Not as long as there's a Holmes to protect her!' Sam yelled as he tackled

Clark. 'There'll always be a Holmes/ Watson team to see that criminals like you never succeed for long.'

Clark and Sam rolled on the ground, each trying to get the upper hand as Jamie moved away from the combatants. She yelled for help and looked for a way to assist Sam against Clark.

As she saw Clark grab the fallen knife, Sam punched Clark in the ribs. A grunt and the sound of splintered bones were the only reactions from Clark as he plunged the knife forward at Sam's stomach. Sam grabbed Clark's hand as the knife grazed his side just above the kidney. Clark pulled the blade back for another try.

In pain, and beginning to weaken from blood loss, Sam continued to hold the knife away from his vital areas. Using holds from his baritsu training, Sam slowly bent Clark's hand and arm backward. As they continued to roll on the ground, the inspector and the marshal arrived in time to see both men suddenly collapse and lie still.

Quickly pulling the two unconscious

men apart, Clark and Sam both were found limp and bloody from stab wounds.

'Doctor!' Fox took her uninjured shoulder firmly. 'Sam is still alive, but we need to stop the bleeding. I think that Clark is dead.'

Using torn pieces of cloth, Inspector Johnson bound Jamie's wounded shoulder so she could assist Marshal Fox with Sam while they awaited medical assistance.

'You weren't supposed to be in harm's way, lass,' Johnson commented. 'We knew we would need your expertise before things got settled down this night.'

Her wound bound, Jamie knelt beside her partner. He looked so pale! The marshal had slowed the bleeding, and she was only able to help him slow the loss of blood to a trickle working one-handed.

'Don't you dare die on me, Samuel Holmes!' she ranted at him. 'You're the last of a legacy that needs to keep going.'

With tears flowing freely, she continued, 'You die now, Sam, and I swear that I'll never let you forget it!'

A firm hand gently pulled her away from Sam.

''Ere now, miss,' the female paramedic told her, 'yer part of the job is done. Now it's our turn.'

The paramedics, moving with skill and speed, were soon able to finish stemming the bleeding. They wrapped bandages around his wounded side and placed him on a gurney.

As they place him in the ambulance, the other paramedic told her, 'Get inside, Doctor. We'll take care of your shoulder on the way to hospital, and you can be with your friend for the entire ride.'

32

Days later, her arm still in a sling, Jamie was allowed to visit an awake and alert Samuel Holmes in his hospital room.

'I guess we both got a little banged up this time.' Sam grinned as Jamie sat down in the chair by the bed. 'Are Jimmy and the rest of your family doing okay?'

'My parents were worried until I met them in the waiting room after I was released from surgery. Jimmy's eyes got real big when he saw my sling. James asked if I had heard how you were doing. Alicia had to hold onto Jimmy to keep him from grabbing anyone who looked like a doctor and demanding to find out about his 'Aunt Jamie's policeman friend'. When they said that you were finally out of surgery, Jimmy wanted to know why you were under arrest when the doctor said that you were in a guarded condition.

'When they finally let us see you, I

thought Jimmy was going to be real trouble. He was crying and saying he was going to punish the 'bad man who hurt my friend'.

'When he finally understood that Clark would never be able to harm anyone again, he settled down. He said to tell you that he misses you and to get well soon.'

'Tell him that I miss him, too.' Sam smiled at the thought of his little friend. 'Tell him to ask his parents and grandparents to bring him to see me as soon as the doctors will allow him to come.'

'That should cheer him up a lot.' Jamie lowered her eyes as she told him, 'Seeing you doing so well has brightened my day, too.'

'It means a lot to me to know that you weren't too badly injured.' Sam reached out and touched her cheek. 'They told me that you worked a minor miracle getting the bleeding to stop. Thank you for my life.'

'As long as there is a Holmes/Watson team,' Jamie paraphrased his remarks from that night, 'there will always be the one to protect the other and to see that criminals like Clark will never succeed for long.'

★　★　★

After Sam's release from the hospital, he was invited to stay at the bee farm where his illustrious ancestor had thought to retire. Marshal Fox had returned with his prisoners to the United States.

Shirley and Bubba, a.k.a. Greco, had been given dates for their hearings. There had been talk of some leniency for their turning state's evidence against the Browns and the BBs.

'Everybody's pointing fingers at everyone else,' Captain Reynolds told them during a conference call. 'You'll be getting more information as things progress. Meanwhile, you and Jamie recuperate and get home as soon as you can. Crime waits for no one and you two have shown yourselves to be the team I thought you would be. Before I forget, someone calling himself 'R.R.' claims that you two owe him a steak dinner with all

338

the trimmings for all of the information he gave you when you return.'

'Our favorite slimeball snitch and his sleazy paper's lead stories,' Jamie laughed. 'We'll be home in our London soon.'

Outside, they overheard Jimmy tell his friends, with pride, 'When I get big, I'm gonna be a detective just like my Aunt Jamie and my friend Sam.'

Sam and Jamie smiled at one another. They, and Jamie's family, silently agreed that the legacy would continue into the next generation.

We do hope that you have enjoyed reading this large print book.

Did you know that all of our titles are available for purchase?

We publish a wide range of high quality large print books including:
Romances, Mysteries, Classics
General Fiction
Non Fiction and Westerns

Special interest titles available in large print are:
The Little Oxford Dictionary
Music Book, Song Book
Hymn Book, Service Book

Also available from us courtesy of Oxford University Press:
Young Readers' Dictionary
(large print edition)
Young Readers' Thesaurus
(large print edition)

For further information or a free brochure, please contact us at:
Ulverscroft Large Print Books Ltd.,
The Green, Bradgate Road, Anstey,
Leicester, LE7 7FU, England.
Tel: (00 44) 0116 236 4325
Fax: (00 44) 0116 234 0205

DARK JOURNEY

Catriona McCuaig

Midwife Maudie Bryant is used to stumbling across murder — but now that she is the mother of a little boy, she has vowed to leave any future crime-solving to her husband Dick, a policeman. However, death strikes too close to home when a wealthy local woman, Cora Beasley, is found strangled with a belt from Maudie's dress. To make matters worse, it is well known that Maudie believed 'the beastly woman was out to snare Dick'. Can Detective Sergeant Bryant help to solve the crime before Maudie is charged as a suspect?

SHERLOCK HOLMES VS. FRANKENSTEIN

David Whitehead

An intriguing mystery lures Sherlock Holmes from the comfort of Baker Street in the winter of 1898: the ghastly murder of a gravedigger in the most bizarre of circumstances. Soon Holmes and Watson are travelling to the tiny German village of Darmstadt, to unmask a callous killer with an even more terrifying motive . . . In nearby Schloss Frankenstein, the eponymous family disowns the rumours attached to its infamous ancestor. But the past cannot be erased, and an old evil is growing strong once again — in the unlikeliest of guises . . .

THE RADIO RED KILLER

Richard A. Lupoff

Veteran broadcaster 'Radio Red' Bob Bjorner is the last of the red-hot lefties working at radio station KRED in Berkeley. His paranoia makes him lock his studio against intruders while he's on the air — but his precaution doesn't save him from a horrible death that leaves him slumped at the microphone just before his three o'clock daily broadcast. Homicide detective Marvia Plum scrambles to the station to investigate. Who amongst the broadcasters, engineers, and administrators present at the station was the murderer — and why?

THE BIG FELLOW

Gerald Verner

Young Inspector Jim Holland of Scotland Yard is under particular pressure to bring to justice 'The Big Fellow' — the mastermind behind a gang committing ever more audacious outrages. As the newspapers mount virulent attacks on Scotland Yard for failing to deal with the rogues, and the crimes escalate from robbery to brutal murder, Holland finds not only his own life threatened, but also that of his theatre actress girlfriend, Diana Carrington.

BLING-BLING, YOU'RE DEAD!

Geraldine Ryan

When the manager of newly-formed girl band Bling-Bling needs a Surveillance Operator to protect them, retired policeman Bill Muir jumps at the chance — but he doesn't know what he's let himself in for . . . In *Making Changes*, Tania Harkness is on a mission to turn around her run-down estate. But someone else is equally determined to stop her . . . And in *Another Country*, Shona Graham returns to her native Orkney island of Hundsay to put right a wrong that saw her brother ostracised by the community many years perviously . . .